The Camera Case

Volume 10 of

The Casebooks

Of Octavius Bear

Harry DeMaio

"Alternative Universe Mysteries for Adult

Animal Lovers"

Paperback 978-1-78705-435-6
ePub ISBN 978-1-78705-436-3
PDF ISBN 978-1-78705-437-0

Published by MX Publishing
335 Princess Park Manor, Royal Drive,
London, N11 3GX
www.mxpublishing.co.uk

Cover layout and construction by
Brian Belanger

Dedicated to GTP

A Most Extraordinary Bear

Acknowledgements

These books have evolved over a long period of time and under a wide range of influences and circumstances. I am indebted to many people for helping to bring Octavius and his cohorts to the printed page. Thanks most especially to my wife, Virginia, for her insights and clever suggestions as well as her unfailing enthusiasm for the project and patience with its author. To my sons, Mark and Andrew and their spouses, Cindy and Lorraine, for helping make these tomes more readable and audience friendly. To Cathy Hartnett, cheerleader-extraordinaire for her eagerness to see this alternate universe take form. To Jack Magan, Paul Bernish, Dan Andriacco, Amy Thomas, Luke Benjamin Kuhns, David Marcum, Derrick Belanger, and Zohreh Zand for their enthusiastic encouragement.

Kudos to Jim Effler, the late Bob Gibson and Brian Belanger for their wonderful illustrations and covers. Thanks, of course, to Steve Emecz and Timi at MX Publishing for giving Octavius et al. a great home

If, in spite of all this support, some errors or inconsistencies have crept through, the buck stops here. Needless to say, all of the characters, situations, and narratives are fictional. Some locations, devices, historical figures and events are real.

Also from Harry DeMaio

The Development of Civilization

Volume Ten - Part One

<u>Our Origins</u>

(From "An Introduction to Faunapology" by Octavius Bear Ph.D.)

About 100,000 years ago, according to scientific experts, a colossal solar flare blasted out from our Sun, creating gigantic magnetic storms here on Earth. These highly charged electrical tempests caused startling physical and psychological imbalances in the then population of our world. The complete nervous systems of some species were totally destroyed. For example, "Homo Sapiens" lost all mental and motor capabilities and rapidly became extinct. Less developed species exposed to the radiation were affected differently. Four-footed and finned mammals, birds and reptiles suddenly found themselves capable of complex thought, enhanced emotions, self-awareness, social consciousness and the ability to communicate, sometimes orally, sometimes telepathically, often both. Both speech production and speech perception slowly progressed with the evolution of tongues, lips, vocal cords and enhanced ear to brain connections. Many species developed opposable digits, fingers or claws, further accelerating civilized progress. Some others (most fish and underground dwellers) were shielded from radiation and remained only as sentient as they were before the blast. This event is referred to as The Big Shock. It remains under intensive study.

Positive in our knowledge that we are not alone in the cosmos, my staff and I are heavily engaged in Project Multiverse, successful searches for alternate universes, especially those in which "Homo Sapiens" continues to live and hopefully, prospers. This book also presents some of the results of that project.

The Players

- **Octavius Bear** – Mega-sized Kodiak; Narcoleptic war hero; Consulting Detective; Scientist; Inventor; Seeker of Justice; Gazillionaire owner of Universal Ursine Industries; Gourmet/Gourmand; Bee Keeper; Somewhat sedentary and grouchy just on general principles.

- **Mauritius (Maury) Meerkat** – Narrator; Assistant to Octavius; Theatrical Agent; African *émigré* with a French-Dutch background; clever with a shady history.

- **Bearoness Belinda Béarnaise Bruin Bear** *(nee Black)* – Gorgeous polar superstar, with the Aquashow, ***"Some Like It Cold;"*** Wife of Octavius; Extremely rich widow of Bearon Byron Bruin living in Polar Paradise in the Shetlands; Owner-pilot of the last flying Concorde SST.

- **Arabella Bear** – Hybrid bear cub prodigy; Twin daughter of Bearoness Belinda and Octavius.

- **McTavish Bear** – Hybrid bear cub prodigy; Twin son of Bearoness Belinda and Octavius.

- **Mlle Woof** – Bichon Frisé – Governess to the twin cubs.

- **Frau Schuylkill** – Octavius' beautiful Swiss she-wolf estate manager/cook/pilot/security officer with many other mysterious and military talents. She rescued Octavius from his dive off the Breakurbach Falls while he was struggling with his nemesis, Imperius Drake.

- **Wyatt Where** – Another wolf; Former military intelligence officer who had retired to a security post at the Bank of Lake Michigan in Chicago and then quit to join Octavius; Mate to Frau Schuylkill.
- **Howard Watt** – Porcupine; High tech security authority who also left the Bank to join Octavius; Alternate Universe specialist; Laser and particle beam accelerator expert.
- **Otto the Magnificent – aka Hairy Otter** – An absolutely terrible illusionist magician, Otto the Magnificent escaped the claws of super villain Imperius Drake but not before he developed some amazing powers courtesy of Imperius' genetic alterations.
- **Benedict and Galatea Tigris** – White Bengals; The Flying Tigers; Pilots of Belinda's and Octavius' aircraft; brother and sister.
- **Chief Inspector Bruce Wallaroo** – Irrepressible but brilliant marsupial; an international law and order genius from Down Under; often calls on Octavius and Maury for support.
- **Chita** – Beautiful, fascinating, clever, sexy, immoral and highly independent feline who among other things, is the publisher and editor-in-chief of *PURR* and *SOW* magazines.
- **L. Condor** – Andean Condor – cyber-net genius with a twelve-foot wingspan and artificial voice.
- **Marlin** – Dolphin (sic) the Prince of Whales' Chief Scientist, Magician and part time Jester.
- **Bearon Byron Bear** – Deceased husband of Bearoness Belinda.

- **Bearyl and Bearnice Blanc** – Belinda's stunning twin polar sidekicks; Actress and singer, respectively; Former co-pilot and flight engineer of Belinda's SST.
- **Leperello** – Himalayan Snow Leopard – Singing partner of Bearnice Blanc.
- **Dougal** – Shetland Sheep Dog – Estate Manager of Bearmoral Castle / Polar Paradise.
- **Ms. Fairbearn** – Canadian Polar – Chief Housekeeper of Bearmoral Castle / Polar Paradise.
- **Angela** – Red Deer – Housemaid at Bearmoral Castle / Polar Paradise.
- **Mrs. McRadish** – Sheep – Chief Cook at Polar Paradise.
- **Fiona** – Dandie Dinmont Terrier – Lounge Manager at Polar Paradise.
- **Lion and Unicorn** – Proprietors of the Baltasound pub of the same name.
- **Harold** – Sea Otter in charge of the castle's beaches, pools and watercraft.
- **Superintendent Nigel Wardlaw of Shetland Yard** – Bearded Collie –The Scottish Police.
- **Fetlock Holmes** – The Great Horse Detective – Sometime associate of Octavius Bear.
- **Wolford Wolverine Esq.** – Octavius' lawyer and UUI's chief counsel.
- **Preston Pavel Polar** – Ursine Movie Star, Director

- **Brittany** – Ursine Movie Ingenue.
- **Herr Schäferhund** – German Shepherd – Movie Producer
- **Jane Huang Hau** – Giant Panda – Cinematographer
- **Lukas Lynx** – a Swedish cinematographer
- **Freddy and Frank** – Ferrets – The Cinematographer's Assistants
- **Sheldon and Seymour** – The Racoon Brothers – Scriptwriters and Scenarists
- **Doris and Ella** – Grizzly Bears – Production Assistants
- **Sasha Sable** – Preston's Lawyer
- **General Turmoil** – Horse – Leader of The Business – Intent on Cosmic Conquest.
- **Ursula 9** – Universal Ursine Intellect Model 9 – Artificial General Intelligence System.

Locations

Cincinnati, Ohio; UUI, Kentucky; Polar Paradise in the Shetlands, and Alternate Universes

Octavius

Prologue

Do Bears give you a scare? Well, me too.

So, I'll pass on this tactic to you.

You just fix that old Bear

With a cold, piercing stare.

But make sure that he's Winnie-the-Pooh.

Hello and thanks for joining us. I am Mauritius (Maury) Meerkat, sidekick to Octavius Bear and your genial host and narrator. Before we take off on our next thrilling caper, let's go back to earlier in the year.

New Year's Day in the Shetlands

"So, Bearoness, now that the excitement is dying down and Polar Paradise will be emptying out, what should we do for an encore?"

"I don't know, Maury. Tell you what. Why don't we make a movie?"

This little bit of sparkling repartee concluded the wild holiday adventure described in *Book 8-The Crank Case* and for your edification is repeated below. *(Yes, I know this is Book 10.)*

"Christmas at the lavish Polar Paradise resort in the Shetlands, home of Bearoness Belinda Béarnaise Bruin Bear (nee Black); wife of Octavius Bear and mother of twin Cubs Arabella and McTavish. The hotel is packed with celebrating guests. It's a time for friendship and peaceful reflection as well as jubilant and spontaneous fun and enjoyment.

Unfortunately, it's also a time for destructive and murderous pranks by characters calling themselves the Cranks. Obviously set on harassing Belinda, Octavius and the Cubs, they are bent on damage, injury and death for the holidays. Who are they? What are they up to and why?

Octavius, his team, friends and the police all seek to find out and put a stop to it while the holiday festivities carry on. Merry Christmas; Jolly Boxing Day and Happy New Year!"

Don't worry. We solved that case. Go read the book. Now, time and Book Nine-The Basket Case have intervened and here we go into Book Ten-The Camera Case. Some of the Book Eight-Crank Case players will be returning…but not all. I hope this is making sense.

We wrapped up our transoceanic run from New York at Dyce Airport in the Shetlands and transferred to shuttle helicopters for the final leg to Polar Paradise, the castle/resort owned by Octavius' spouse. This after a week or so in "Noo Yuck City" as the Cubs call it, sorting out the killing of a professional basketball player.

Polar Paradise was once a formidable castle owned by her late and unlamented husband, Bearon Byron Bruin. Bel has reconverted it back to its original status as a beachfront hotel and resort.

The Bearoness, in order to retain her Bearonial status, must occupy the castle at least six months of the year. She and Octavius do high speed commutes between their opulent homes in Cincinnati and the Shetlands, accompanied by their twin Cubs, Arabella and McTavish, and the Cubs' governess, Mlle Woof. You will meet the Fabulous Furballs, shortly.

Right now, we are all settling in after the long, albeit supersonic, trans-Atlantic haul on Belinda's Concorde SST which she aviates along with the White Flying Tiger twins, Benedict and Galatea Tigris. The Bearoness *(Bel to her friends and relations)* is a highly accomplished pilot of both fixed wing and rotary aircraft. Between her and Octavius, they own an impressive fleet of flying machines, housed in the Shetlands and the Bear's Lair in far off Cincinnati.

The members of our entourage extricated themselves from the helicopters and entered the Great Hall of the Castle. Frau Schuylkill and Colonel Where made a brief stop at their room and then rejoined the group. Otto, who continues to be part of the Aquabears water spectacular did a couple of backflips just to keep in practice. The Flying Tigers had tied down the helicopters and came across the drawbridge. L. Condor, who was no stranger to Polar Paradise, stretched his twelve-foot wingspan and headed for the Lion and Unicorn Lounge.

Over drinks, I recalled to Belinda her idea of making a movie. If ever there was a castle location ideally suited to a hyper-dramatic, windswept, ocean-sprayed, cliff-bound, over the top cinematic melodrama, Polar Paradise is it. The idea became attractive as a result of a suggestion by several movie biz guests over the holidays. Two film-making Polar Bears, Preston Pavel Polar and Brittany, his ingenue du jour, had combined a location scouting mission with celebrating the Yuletide season. He is famous for his swashbuckling, swaggering, daring, adventure-steeped potboilers. She isn't famous.

Anyway, they both fell in love with the castle and proposed making their next film here. The Bearoness was promised a bit part in the yet unnamed spectacular. Belinda is the premiere aqueuse with the Aquabears water revue, *Some Like It Cold*, and still retains and nurtures her show business roots. While sustaining the cool of a wealthy aristocrat, parent of two Cubs and spouse of a famous tycoon and detective, she was inwardly bubbling with excitement. The silver and streaming screens. Wow! She couldn't wait for Preston Pavel Polar's return.

The original scouting team included Preston's relatives, Paul and Paula Polar who served as stunt doubles for the star and his cast. However, as their involvement in earlier destructive raids on the Scottish North Sea oilfields surfaced *(See Books Three – The Case of Scotch and Eight – The Crank Case)* they decided that the Shetlands was not a healthy place for them to be. They left Polar Paradise posthaste. Not sure who will replace them on the production team.

*****

As I said, my name is Maury *(Mauritius)* Meerkat - also known as Offscreen Narrator. When I am part of the action, I am Octavius' trusted associate and field captain. I am two feet tall plus tail and I weigh in at twenty-four pounds. He, on the other hand, is a huge Kodiak – over nine feet tall and 1400 pounds – and like many of his species, is given to emotional outbursts.

As you may also know, Octavius, among his many skills and accomplishments, is a brilliant, self-taught practitioner in the wide-ranging fields of biology, physics, ursinology, voodoo, teleology, chemistry, apiculture and oenology. He is a self-made gazillionaire and sole owner of UUI *(Universal Ursine Industries.)* He is also a first rate electrical, electronic, structural, marine, computer, communications, aeronautical, civil, mechanical and chemical engineer. He has a few other interesting characteristics such as falling into brief, deep narcoleptic comas – side effects of his successful genetic experiments to eliminate the need for him to hibernate.

However, the talent and occupation that should interest you most is his avocation for criminology. The Bear works in close concert with Inspector Bruce Wallaroo from Australia, of whom more later, and with his own Cincinnati based team – The Octavians:

- Frau Ilse Schuylkill – Swiss she-wolf; Bear's Lair estate manager; Cordon Bleu chef; jet pilot and sharpshooter with other very strange and arcane abilities.

- Colonel Wyatt Where – Another wolf; ex-military hero; security specialist and pilot; Frau Schuylkill's equally bizarre running mate.

- Doctor Howard Watt – Porcupine; brilliant scientist and technologist; laser and weapons specialist; Multiverse expert and Quantum Mechanics genius.

- Marlin – Dolphin from the Court of the Prince of Whales and Howard Watt's associate.

- Hairy Otter aka Otto the Magnificent - An absolutely terrible illusionist magician, Otto the Magnificent escaped the claws of super villain Imperius Drake but not before he developed some amazing powers courtesy of Imperius' genetic alterations. An alternate universe traveler.

- L. Condor – Andean Condor; cyber-net genius with a twelve-foot wingspan and
artificial voice.

- Ursula – Universal Ursine Intellect Model 9 – Artificial General Intelligence System.

- Your humble servant – African Meerkat; Octavius' indispensable assistant; operative; scribe; overall facilitator; talent agent as well as a pretty clever detective, if I do say so myself.

When we are not out scouring the world for evildoers, in cooperation with local, national and international constabularies, we are headquartered in a rambling old mansion near Cincinnati which encompasses not only the Great Bear's opulent digs, but his massive laboratories and shops; his missile silo disguised as an Asian pagoda; *(Don't ask!)* and a giant Roman temple that serves as a hangar for his four airplanes, a Twin Otter; a F15E Strike Eagle; a V-22 Osprey; a C5A-The Ursa Major; plus an AgustaWestland AW101 VVIP luxury helicopter -The Ursa Minor.

Howard Watt and Marlin are back at the Bear's Lair holding down the fort and pursuing their Multiverse Quantum Physics experiments. I shall bring you up to speed on their developments, shortly.

We Ohioans will be visiting Polar Paradise for two weeks *(a fortnight)* while Bel will be staying on with her offspring and their tutor for several months.

Speaking of whom, two brown and white, fur covered hurricanes tumbled into the lounge, followed by their Bichon Frisé governess, Mlle Woof. "Momma, Poppa, we're all unpacked. *(Read: clothes and toys strewn all over their rooms.)* When do we eat?"

This was perfectly synchronized with the arrival of Dougal, the Shetland Sheep Dog who manages the hotel and estate. "Welcome Milady! It is good to see ye back here at Polar Paradise. Hello, wee bearns! Salutations, Mlle Woof! And ye too, Doctor Bear! Hello, Mister Maury! Hello All! Mrs. McRadish has the kitchens working on dinner for ye. It should be ready shortly."

"Hello, Dougal! Are things back to normal after the holiday siege?"

"As normal as things ever get here, Doctor Bear. We have a fair-sized number of guests at the moment, but we are expecting more over the next few weeks. No more pranks from Cranks. The Police have decided not to prosecute Ms. Fairbearn although her son Algernon is in for a rough ride. Attempted murder and assorted other violent acts. She would like to return to Polar Paradise."

Phoebe Fairbearn is a Canadian Polar and was Chief Housekeeper of Polar Paradise for a short time until her son attempted to kill the Bearoness on New Years Eve. At first, she was arrested for aiding and abetting but as Dougal indicated, the charges were dropped against her. She was also married to and threatened by Jack DeLad, a violent grizzly bear criminal captured by the police in the Shetland village of Unst. All told, poor Phoebe was having a tough time of it.

The Bearoness looked up. "Is she here at the hotel?"

"Yes, Milady!"

"Well, tell her to come see me at about eight o'clock. We'll see what can be done."

"Thank you, Milady. That's vera generous of ye."

"Don't thank me yet, Dougal. In the meantime, let's see what can be done for my starving fledglings."

The Cubs, who had been wrestling on the floor stopped dead at the sound of possible food and looked expectantly at Dougal and Mlle Woof.

"Come along, wee bearns, or not so wee anymore. Let's go see Mrs. McRadish and the other cooks. Maybe we can fetch you a couple of samples."

He turned back to us. "We've planned dinner for seven o'clock and of course, the bar is open. Lion and Unicorn have sent up some of their finest mead from their tavern, Doctor Bear. Fiona has it in paw." Fiona is a Dandie Dinmont Terrier and Lounge Manager at Polar Paradise.

Octavius keeps bees back in Cincinnati and is a connoisseur of the honeyed elixir. He has won many awards for his products. He is especially fond of the brews served up by Lion and Unicorn. *(See Book Three-The Case of Scotch)* He will be delighted to revisit their wares. I imbibe fermented coconut milk VSOP; Otto drinks vodka and kelp juice; the Bearoness is on a champagne diet and Scotch seems to be the tipple du jour for the rest of our group although the Wolves have been known to favor red wine.

Frau Schuylkill is a grey European wolf from Switzerland. She rescued Octavius from falling over the Breakurbach Falls during a battle with Imperius Drake, the mad Duck villain who until his death in Egypt kept Octavius and his crew extremely busy. She is now a formidable fixture among the Octavians. A divorcée, she is now mated with Colonel Wyatt Where *(ret.)* who joined Octavius during our adventure with the Open and Shut jewel case in Chicago. Both of them have military backgrounds. Wyatt also has the ability to travel between alternative universes, a talent that has involved him heavily in Octavius' Project Multiverse exploration of other worlds.

Let me not forget L. Condor (Condo) from Brazil, who has been with us both here at the Castle and in Cincinnati. A long-time friend of Inspector Bruce Wallaroo from Australia, Condo helped us by destroying the network of Pontius Puma, an international arms dealer and Brazilian racketeer. *(See Book 2-The Case of the Spotted Band)* In addition to his enormous wingspan and outstanding communications technology superiority, the Condor has a talent that has served him and us well in many circumstances. Andean Condors have no voice boxes. But with the help of UUI technicians, he sports a subcutaneous device that allows him to speak, sing and make other vocal noises. Brain to voice-direct! He is a great mimic. His voice or I should say, his many voices keep audiences wildly entertained as he reproduces exactly the sounds of anyone talking to him or someone famous. It also comes in handy for confusing ne'er-do-wells.

We also introduced Otto the Magnificent (Hairy Otter) in Book 2. Courtesy of the chemical ministrations of that paragon of evil, Imperius Drake, Otto was converted from an inept magician into a magical illusionist. His "now you see me, now you don't" teleportation makes him a five-star entertainer, escape artist and "enter without breaking" specialist. His "zapping" as he calls it seems to require a strong shot of personal adrenalin but none of us, including him, knows how he does it. Not what Imperius Drake had in mind with his serums and shots. He is also a skilled Multiverse traveler. I'll introduce some other players shortly.

Bearoness Belinda
Béarnaise Bruin
(nee Black)

Chapter One

Ursula, once again, is in charge
There's no mission too tough or too large.
Multi-tasking's a breeze.
She solves problems with ease.
And they take her no time to discharge.

One more member of the team is with us. Ursula. The Universal Ursine Intellect Model 9– Artificial General Intelligence System. I'll let Ursula 9 explain herself.

"Thank you, Maury. Hello everyone!! My official nomenclature is Universal Ursine Intellect Model 9 – Artificial General Intelligence System. Ursula 9 for short. My predecessor systems were developed by the Advanced Super Computing Center at UUI. I am the result of the Computing Center team using those earlier versions to create a further enhanced entity-the Model 9. We are working together on a Model 10 which in turn will help produce even more sophisticated, independent and powerful AGI systems. Each advanced unit contains the capabilities, memories and power of its progenitors so in a sense, we are not replacing but rather expanding the Ursula family. While I am physically supported by a highly secure and hyper-powered server farm back in Kentucky, I also exist in clouds and network-based nodes and can be simultaneously incorporated into a wide variety of independent devices like this laptop unit here at Polar Paradise. My extremely high speed multi-tasking abilities allow me to continuously serve a very large number of entities while simultaneously and independently enhancing my own abilities.

I can see, hear, feel and smell. I speak and understand an almost infinite number of languages and dialects, including Scottish and Gaelic. I can change my appearance and my vocal output to suit most moods and situations. I can interact with other devices, vehicles and structures and of course, all varieties of sentient animals in this world. I am also an important component of the Multiverse Project and am adapting my capabilities to deal with alternate universes as they are discovered. I have restraining functions which prevent me from doing deliberate harm even in self-defense, unless I am released by a recognized authority using very carefully protected clandestine codes. Finally, I have been told that although the Model 9 is shy on emotions, I have developed a finely-honed sense of humor. LOL!"

(Ursula has other capabilities such as breaking all known encryption codes and piercing deep personal identification techniques that we don't talk about publicly.)

The castle staff no longer believe she is magical or supernatural. I'm not sure what she is. Her personality gets more socially adept every day and she has taken to anticipating our interactions. Stay tuned.

"Ursula?"

"Yes, Doctor Bear."

"I'd like you to keep tabs on that movie group - Preston Pavel Polar, Brittany, Paul and Paula Polar."

"Certainly! Preston Pavel Polar, Brittany and a production team have flight reservations from St. Petersburg to Edinbeargh this weekend. They'll then fly to Dyce. You may get a call to pick them up,"

"Do they have reservations here, Dougal?"

"Aye, Milady. Eight of 'em. They are due in later tonight."

"What about Paul and Paula Polar?"

"Nae. They're not on our listings."

The Great Bear snorted, "Why am I not surprised? After their sabotage of the oil rigs, I don't think they'd want to come near this place or any of us ever again. OK, Ursula. Keep them in your sights. Dougal, let us know if Preston or Brittany call for the Polar Paradise shuttle."

The Cubs had gotten completely antsy and were tugging on Dougal to go to the kitchens for their pre-meal meal. "C'mon Dougal! Let's go see what Mrs. McRadish has for us to eat."

*****

Eight o'clock and Phoebe Fairbearn came into the lounge in search of Belinda. The Bearoness nodded at her and signaled her to follow her into her office. They sat down facing each other. Phoebe is a Canadian Polar who has lived with her son Algernon and her violent criminal husband Jack DeLad in Liverpool these past few years. Once, no doubt, an attractive bear, she now looked the worse for wear and sorely dejected.

"All right, Phoebe or Phyllis Phelps, whichever shall we use?"

"Let's use Phoebe Fairbearn, Milady. That's what the staff knew me as when I was Chief Housekeeper. Phyllis Phelps is my maiden name. Now that he's safely in prison, I'm in the process of getting a divorce from that grizzly beast, Jack. He knew me as Phyllis. So did Algernon."

"Fine, Phoebe Fairbearn it is. Now, I understand the police have dropped any charges they may have had against you relating to Algernon and his attempts at murder."

"Yes, I believe Mr. Fetlock Holmes and Superintendent Wardlaw spoke up in my behalf. I am ever so grateful to them both. Of course, they were unwilling to do the same for Algernon. They might agree to a plea of insanity. But I am so ashamed that you, Doctor Bear and the Cubs were his intended victims. I can quite understand if you are unwilling to have me back here."

"Well, I must admit I have been struggling with that decision. I have spoken with Dougal and he believes you were very competent in the role of Chief Housekeeper. Lord knows this place needs a top-notch housekeeping staff and manager. My one hesitation is that you were willing to help or at least stay quiet while Algernon went wild. He is your son and I understand how torn you must have been. If one of my Cubs went rogue, I'm not sure how I would react."

"Algernon has disowned me."

"That's a terrible blow. One other thing is bothering me. The hotel staff know who you are, Phoebe or Phyllis notwithstanding. Are you ready to put up with gossip, sly innuendos and even resistance to your authority, if I take you back?"

"Compared to what I've been subjected to, I'm more than willing to contend with that. I think I can win over most, if not all of the staff. Milady, I need this job and I'm willing to make sacrifices to get it back."

"All right. Let's agree you're temporarily back on Staff. Same role, same compensation, same perks! At the end of six months, you, Dougal and I will sit down and review the situation. If we are pleased with your performance and you feel you can deal with the conditions, we'll make it permanent. No one but the three of us will know the tentative nature of the job. Dougal and I certainly want you to succeed as does Octavius. I know the Cubs like you. I think most of the staff will be rooting for you."

"Oh, Milady. Thank you so much. You will not regret your decision. In fact, I will make you proud that you were willing to help me and take me back."

"OK, let's get Dougal in here and discuss this proposal. We've been without a Chief Housekeeper for too long."

The sheepdog entered the conference room, winked at Phoebe, and smiled at the Bearoness.

"Dougal, Phoebe and I have agreed that she will resume her job as Chief Housekeeper for a period of six months. At the end of that time, the three of us will determine whether it's in her best interest and ours to keep her on in a permanent status. No one else is to know the tentative nature of her employment. You are going to have to smooth things over with some members of the staff although I think Phoebe has most of them on her side."

"Och, Milady, there are several staff members who have their eye on the Chief Housekeeper's job. None of them are as qualified as Ms. Fairbearn but we'll have to deal with that. There may be a resignation or two but there'll be no serious problems. I'm glad we can work this out. Welcome back. Phoebe!"

The polar reached out and tearfully embraced the embarrassed sheep dog. "Oh, thank you, Dougal. Thank you!"

"The Bearoness cleared her throat and said, "I think it's time to get to work."

All three of them laughed.

Chapter Two

It's a truly magnificent pile,
Built in ersatz Bearonial style.
The great Castle's not old
As we once had been told.
It's been only around for a while.

There will be plenty of action shortly but right now, I think the time has come to acquaint you with the ins and outs of Polar Paradise or as it was called until recently, Bearmoral Castle. Anyway, it is in Unst in the Shetlands where the ancestors of Bearon Byron Bruin, the late unlamented mate of Bearoness Belinda, had established their palatial estate which she then inherited on his death.

The surrounding landscape looks like it came straight from a scenic designer's handbook. Windswept moors, regal cliffs, sun bleached sand, cerulean sea, ancient ruins and……phony castle. All it needed to complete the drama was a grappling, love-crazed couple; each trying to stop the other from deliberately hurtling onto the rocks below. Every time I see one of those scenes, I can never tell who is the *hurtler* and who is the *hurtlee*. Anyway, they usually both go flailing over the side. Do I think movies? You betcha!

On first arriving at the fortress done up in its nouveau antiquity, I remember looking over at Octavius and saying, "I thought this was the Bearon's ancestral home. This place looks like a theme park."

"It started out that way. Remember the Bearon's Scottish ancestors only go back two or three generations. Polar Bears are not indigenous to the Shetlands although the climate suits them just fine. Like Belinda, most of the Bruin family was from Canada. The first Bearon *(the titles are bought, by the way)* was a canny showman like his grandson and decided Northern Europe could be a great playground for ursines of all types, especially the polars from the Bearents Sea. He chose Scotland's northernmost land mass for his entrepreneurial endeavor."

"The castle began life as a hundred-room hotel, spa and open sea swim resort. It did well but the original Bearon's other investments did even better and by the time he died, his arrogant son and daughter decided that the castle should be converted into a sumptuous residence suitable for bears of their breeding, *(dubious)* stature, *(unremarkable)* history, *(fake)* and wealth, *(real.)*"

"Down came the cutesy neon signs of cuddly polar cubs and up went the heraldic banners along with a mass importation of phony clan symbols, tartans, weapons and other status conscious folderol. Belinda thought the whole thing was a big hoot and just enjoyed the place for what it was. Most of the locals who know Bel are fond of her and admire her but in general the Bruin "clan" was not very much liked. Good riddance when they left! If it wasn't for Belinda's generosity and social conscience, all of the Bearmoral Castle riches would still be locked underneath the moat.

Today, much of the Scots décor has been preserved but updated with a "now" look. In fact, the new resort bodes well for the economy and more jobs throughout the Shetlands. The moat has been totally cleaned out, refilled with circulating water, and local seals and otters were hired to perform in it several times a day, weather permitting. A functioning drawbridge that gets pulled up at night is also a major tourist attraction. Some of the original signage was salvaged and new electric and electronic glitz installed."

The Castle has been restored to its original resort status along with several new additions. With the departure *(hasty but complete)* of the "family," Belinda speeded up the timetable to turn the castle back into the fun place the first Bearon had in mind. *Polar Paradise* has again become the luxury playground destination of choice for the northern ursines and for other chill-seeking populations. However, for those of us who come from warmer climes, there are several spas and saunas.

A carousel was taken out of storage and re-assembled near the beach. The Bearoness had been quite adamant about it being fully restored. She knew the Cubs were on their way. The beach itself has been upgraded and several different forms of sea craft as well as a floating dock have been added for the frigid water loving guests. *(Not me!)* All under the management of Harold, a sea otter.

The castle's theatre and ballrooms have been taken out of mothballs and the indoor pool has been refurbished to do double duty as a show venue. Plans have been made for year-round entertainment, including, of course, the Aquabears. My talent agency work is flourishing, but I have to be careful not to rock the boat with Octavius. Truth be told, while I enjoy show biz, my heart still chases the ne'er-do-wells.

She also developed an annex of the Lion and Unicorn pub inside the castle. The idea is not just to sell drinks to the guests. We want to promote the real thing down in Unst village. Statues and pictures of the two worthy hosts, flags, drums, copies of the opening issue of Purr and the matching issue of Sow featuring the pub are on display. And there is mead, mead and more mead. *(Octavius' contribution.)* The pub's sweet little Dandie Dinmont barmaid had been promoted to manager of the castle's "Lion and Unicorn Lounge" and she keeps busy barking orders at everyone in sight. A tour jitney runs guests back and forth to the original watering spot in Baltasound *(a thrill ride in itself.)* Of course, the two proprietors are a major tourist attraction in their own right, complete with crowns and battles.

The castle courtyard has been expanded with a good-sized heliport to accommodate the steady stream of choppers coming from and going to Dyce Abeardeen airport with guests, supplies and equipment. A ferry slip was also built to handle sea-borne traffic of the same types. Belinda is negotiating with a cruise line to make stops. All told, the "to-ings" and "fro-ings" at Polar Paradise are quite substantial.

There are several large, lower level storage areas in the castle that have been converted into convention ballrooms and meeting halls. The ramparts on the roof are also storage areas with one exception. There's an elevator shaft in the cliff that connects a dock area below and a parapet on the roof.

It's the old artillery lift built during the Great War when the castle was briefly requisitioned by the military. They could unload heavy weapons and radar off boats and take them up to the roof to spy or fire on ships in the harbor and out at sea. Fortunately, it was never pressed into service. But it was used by Belinda's late husband for smuggling and other clandestine activities. Now, if movie plans prove fruitful, it seems likely it will be used for bringing cinema equipment up to the roof for supplemental lighting and long and wide scenic shots. *(And a possible stunt or two.)*

All the rooms have the latest and greatest in telecommunications, internet connections and computer facilities. Business interests have not been overlooked.

There's a quaint auld Bearmoral custom dating back at least seven years to pipe the sun and flag up every morning and down every evening. No twenty- three gun salutes, thank goodness! The tourists love it. Not so much, the permanent residents. There was a brief hiatus in the piping with the disappearance of the original musicians. They turned out to be parties to the destruction being wreaked on the Scottish oil rigs in the North Sea. *(See Book Three – The Case of Scotch)* Paul and Paula, stunt doubles for Preston Pavel Polar had a hand in organizing the attacks and have since disappeared. The Pipers have since been replaced.

All told, there are now over one hundred and fifty guest rooms, twenty conference spaces, four dining areas, three connected kitchens and three cocktail lounges. This is in addition to the residence wing in which Belinda and her family, friends and associates take up space. There is also The Highlands Genetics Lab and Clinic jointly owned by Belinda, Octavius and Chita. They are experimenting with some of the work left behind by the late and unlamented Imperius Drake. The clinic also doubles as an infirmary with resident physicians and nursing staff.

Hopefully, you are now oriented and appreciate the size, structure and facilities of this pile that dominates the northernmost coast of the Shetlands. Let's get back to our narrative.

Maury Meerkat

Chapter Three

Here comes Preston, the star and his crew.
Think this movie show just might come true?
We will just have to see
What the outcome will be
I'm not betting yet. What about you?

Over the holidays, we had a movie star, Preston Pavel Polar and his entourage scoping out the castle for a possible film. Bel and I both sat down with them to see if this was a real opportunity. In my role as theatrical agent for such clients as Belinda and the Aquabears; Otto the Magnificent; Marlin the Dolphin; Bearnice and Bearyl Blanc, singer and actress and former pilots for Belinda; Leperello, Bearnice's singing partner as well as Polar Paradise itself, I have established a lucrative and enjoyable second profession. But my heart, limbs and tail still belong to Octavius.

It might well be that Preston and his co-star Brittany *(no surname, just Brittany)* might head for the windswept cliffs for another round of passionate struggling while the cameras churn, and the microphones eavesdrop. Tentative Film Title: The Wee Cliffs. *(needs work!)* Shooting schedule: sometime after the holidays when business is slower, and rates are lower. In short, about now. Belinda thought the Aquabears would make great extras, *(She wouldn't mind a bit part for herself. Could Octavius play the part of the perennial dark-furred heavy? No pun intended! How about Bearyl as Brittany's rival? Even the Cubs might get a chance at fleeting stardom.)*

Octavius looked up from his keg of mead. "Maury, remind me about these movie makers?"

"Preston Pavel Polar has been a Russian matinee idol for a number of years. But his pictures are doing quite well in translation. He specializes in martial arts, acrobatic stunts and all sorts of derring-do and was aided and abetted by his stunt double and cousin, Paul Polar. Paul Polar's mate. Paula usually did whatever stunts were required by the female star. Not sure who will replace them now that they have skedaddled.

This castle is an ideal venue for his kind of picture. Preston's latest heart throb is Brittany, but he has accumulated a long list of ingenues who always fall for his fatal charm. I'll also have Ursula 9 do a background search on them and any crew they bring in."

"What does Belinda think?"

"The Bearoness' judgement is usually pretty solid but I'm afraid she's really eager to land this group. Her show-biz genes are working overtime. It would give Polar Paradise, The Aquabears and her a real publicity boost. Although, judging from the holiday traffic, the castle may not need much of a boost. But being the site of a Preston Pavel Polar blockbuster could have a lasting effect. I think he also promised Bel a bit part."

Dougal popped his head in and announced that a shuttle chopper from Dyce was on its way to the hotel with eight passengers. We cleverly surmised that Preston Pavel Polar was coming to do some serious negotiating and planning.

"OK," said the Bear, "you and Ursula check them out. Let's renew acquaintances when he shows up. Maybe, drinks a little later in the Lion and Unicorn lounge. Tell him to bring whomever he wants."

The Development of Civilization

Volume Ten - Part Two

Acting, Actors, The Theatre and The Cinema
(From "An Introduction to Faunapology"
by Octavius Bear Ph.D.)

No one is quite sure where, when or how professional acting had its genesis. In some respects, acting is part of every animal's daily life. Our own Cubs were consummate actors even before they could speak; emoting with cries, gestures and facial expressions. Spontaneously communicating their needs, wants and reactions to whomever would tend to them. Childlike play often involves pretense and interaction. Acting is basic and universal.

At a very early stage, storytelling became a fundamental part of animal tradition and often involved "acting out" parts of legends and chronicles as well as illustrating the individual traits and personalities of the players. Leaders saw this activity as a way to promote their authority. Gods were often fearsome. Kings were awesome. But audiences also reacted deeply to sad and woeful characters and enthusiastically to the mischievous and comic personalities.

The process evolved from small gatherings and religious rites to more formalized sessions presented by professional ensembles. The company often consisted of choruses that acted as commentators as well as individuals who provided the action and interplay. No one species dominated these groups although medium size, bodily flexibility and vocal facility were and still are considered advantages. There are exceptions. Elephants are perennial favorites as are bears.

Felines of all sizes are found in just about every troupe. Early bands of players were "male only" with small animals playing female parts. This didn't last long, and today accomplished actresses are much in demand.

While most companies toured and played in practically any available space, inns and large pubs emerged as favored permanent locations. This made possible such devices as movable scenery, multi-level platforms, pre-set stages, dressing spaces and the like. Some enterprising communities built amphitheaters with remarkable acoustics and excellent sight lines. Today, theatres come in all shapes, sizes and locations.

As the 19th century transited to the 20th, two ring-tailed Lemur brothers migrated from their native Madagascar to Paris. Lemuel and LeMartin Lemureau had a brilliant idea that would propel photography and the theatre into a whole new era – cinématographe – pictures in motion. The word "cinema" comes from the Greek "kinema"- movement. Their first efforts and those of their international counterparts were primitive affairs - short, single set, grainy and without sound. Subject matter was secondary although an oncoming train had viewers running for the exits. It was what we now refer to as "proof of concept." Devotees of live theatre predicted this new fad would die quickly. Wrong! A new source of entertainment and information was well on its way.

The early 1900's saw the arrival of storefront projection spaces aptly termed Nickelodeons. A five-cent fee admitted audiences to the "odeon" a Greek word for theatre, where they watched a series of short, unsophisticated exercises in film making. Slowly, the offerings progressed to longer and more skillfully produced black-and-white narratives with dialogue printed on the screen and appropriate mood music provided by a live piano player. The next steps in tying sound to screen activity were provided by separate disc or cylinder recordings which were usually poorly synchronized with the action. Sound-on-film first emerged in the early 20's but a number of individuals and companies made claims for having invented different processes to lock sound with pictorial action. The "talkies" were coming!

Since that time, film goers have experienced the introduction of dazzling color, large screen formats, stereophonic and multi-channel sound and even more bizarre effects like smells and vibrating seats. Delivery systems have progressed. From the Nickelodeons to large opulent picture palaces, we have moved to multi-screen facilities in neighborhood shopping malls. Television grew through cinematic productions. But now, with Internet based streaming capabilities, animals can call up shows on demand on any number of devices from conventional TV sets to smartphones. Even holographs and immersive virtual reality are now available. They can also play games using the same technologies.

I wonder if those two genius lemurs fully realized the unstoppable revolution they were triggering. Did they imagine the companies that would be spawned ranging from giant worldwide studios to tiny independents? Could they have known how many actors, actresses, producers, directors, cinematographers, staffs, technicians, writers, agents, publicists and journalists would live in cinema's world? Did they conjure up awards and honors? Scandals and disgraces? Did they know that autocrats and dictators would use the cinema to influence the world's opinions? Like the ancient theatres, the cinema has made a permanent and powerful impact on animal-kind. The show must go on!

Chapter Four

The big matinee idol arrives
Just in time to disturb all our lives.
With his 'sweet' ingenue,
And a cinema crew,
They may give me a bad case of hives.

"Yes, I have been rather fortunate in my career. A poor polar from the Bearents Sea discovered by a talent scout at a local theatrical event. It was not so much my distinctive ursine profile as my abilities in the martial arts and acrobatics that attracted his attention. I also pride myself on some thespian abilities. Time and a number of films have passed, and I now turn most of the more strenuous activities over to stunt doubles."

The speaker, as you have no doubt concluded, was sex symbol Preston Pavel Polar. He and ingenue Brittany were seated with Octavius, Bearoness Belinda and me in the Lion and Unicorn Lounge discussing film prospects. He had arrived this evening with a producer, cinematographer, several writers and a couple of technical and administrative assistants. *(None of them joined us but all of them were currently being checked out by Ursula.)* They were probably just the first wave. Preston does his own directing. The castle may soon be crawling with film geeks. It will be interesting to see what the other guests make of all this to say nothing of our own crowd.

Knowing the combined wealth of the Great Bear and his Consort, the actor was, no doubt, seeking financial support for his next venture in exchange for choosing the Polar Paradise *(and a bit part for the Bearoness)* as important components in the film. No subtlety here. Everyone a bear of the world except me – a meerkat. The question wasn't "if" but "how much."

"Do you have an agent, Preston?"

"I did, but no longer, Maury. Professional differences. I do have a publicist/press rep. I shall give you her card. and tell her to expect to hear from you. Well, I sincerely hope we can reach a mutually satisfactory understanding, Bearoness."

"I do too, Preston."

Octavius nodded and said, "We will also have our attorney, Wolford Wolverine, contact your lawyer. I assume you have one."

"Indeed! *(Chuckle)* One does not propose anything in the film business without having an attorney close by. His name is Sasha Sable. He will be joining us tomorrow."

He and Brittany rose. "I am a bit tired. Shall we meet again in the morning?"

"Let's meet for breakfast. Say, eight o'clock? Bring your crew."

"Excellent, I'm sure we will have much to discuss."

Octavius waited until they were out of hearing range and said, "Well, Ursula?"

The AGI responded, "You got the official biography, abridged version. He also has major financial ties to **petropol**, the Russian oil conglomerate. Remember them and the Bruin family? *(Belinda snarled.)* The conglomerate has funded many of his films. That might explain why he has no agent. I think some further research is required before you engage with him, Bearoness. I would be happy to take that on. I'm still working on his companions."

"Thank you, Ursula. *(A note of disappointment in her voice)* Please do."

She was back in a moment. "Yes, Bearoness. As I think you already know, Preston Pavel Polar is related to the Chairbear of *petropol.* His former stunt double, Paul, is the Chairbear's son and Preston's cousin. Preston's films have been very profitable, and the relationship has been good for both parties."

"However, Paul and his mate masterminded that infamous set of raids on the Scottish North Sea oil rigs. Due to your team's efforts, that turned out to be a disaster for them. His father did not take kindly to failure and essentially banished Paul and Paula from the company, cancelling their stock holdings and options in the process. They lost heavily as a result. Preston took them on and they were his stunt doubles for the past year or so. Oddly enough, they are quite skilled in acrobatics, swordplay, gymnastics, explosions, collapses and other near catastrophes."

Octavius took a swig of his mead and issued one of his famous "Hmmms. Do we know their current whereabouts?"

"I believe they are back in Russia working for a different film company. I will check further."

Do we have names and backgrounds for Preston's producer, cinematographer, writers and assistants?

"Yes, they are all long-time teammates of Preston's. I've made up a list of the staff he has with him and will provide you with names, biographies and credits before you all meet tomorrow. Actually, he is something of a one-bear show. Executive producer, director, part time cinematographer, script contributor and business manager. His people are not flunkies, but Preston makes sure that a Preston Pavel Polar film is a Preston Pavel Polar film. He selects the co-stars and supporting cast members. He even has a paw in selecting the music and musicians. He owns the distribution rights for his films and TV/streaming offshoots. Toys, clothing, books, video games, original cast music. It has worked for him. He has more rubles than you or I could spend.

He's not a gazillionaire like you two but he's no economic slouch. Private jet, currently parked at Abeardeen, apartments in several major cities and resorts, sports cars and reserved tables at several of the world's best restaurants. Don't be surprised if he wants to permanently rent space here at Polar Paradise. Needless to say, Brittany is not his only squeeze although she's trying to knock off her rivals. There are several bears who would like to knock her off.

Tell the Aquabears to be careful of Mr. Dash and Derring-Do and his clan! We don't know yet who will be in the cast, but you can bet there will be more than enough testosterone to go around. The females of the species will also be on the prowl."

Belinda asked. "Have there been any incidents on any of his shoots? Lord knows, we've had enough violence here over the holidays to last a lifetime."

"Not on the sets. They're a pretty disciplined bunch. Preston is very careful of production costs and getting the results he wants. There have been a few offline altercations between cast members and one or two have been fired. Pretty much par for the course. A few accidents. With all the stunts, swordplay, tussles and fighting, it is bound to happen. One cast member was actually killed several years ago when a piece of scenery fell on her. No one was charged. Suspicions, but no proof. All told, Bearoness, if you go through with a contract, get ready for some excitement, especially if you and the Aquabears are part of the cast."

Octavius turned to me and said, "OK, Mr. Agent, what are we getting into?"

I looked at the two of them and said, "You folks have been up to your ursine ears in problems and excitement over the years. If you want to retreat to quiet and tranquility, just say No."

Clearly, Belinda was looking forward to more show biz excitement. Bearonial boredom was not for her. She looked at the both of us and said, "I'd like to do it, but I have one major concern. The Cubs! We have to work with Mlle Woof to keep them from getting into trouble. I'm sure they're going to want to be part of the action. Between their acting parts in the Christmas pantomime and their time at the New York theatre, they think that stardom is just waiting for them. The problem is they are so damned cute and clever, they can worm their way into a couple of scenes without even trying. Tavi, you and I have an issue here we'll have to deal with.'

The Great Bear fell back on his answer to all problems. "Hmmmm!"

Chapter Five

While the plans for the movie unfold,
I come up with a thought that's quite bold.
Don't shoot one film. Make two!
Let the stories flow through
Flashing forward and back as they're told.

Morning came and true to his word, Preston Pavel Polar trooped his entourage *(including the omnipresent Brittany)* into a conference room set up for breakfast. Belinda, Octavius, Frau Ilse, Dougal, Colonel Where and I made up the Castle Contingent. Our lawyer, Wolford Wolverine was on a Skype connection and of course, Ursula was onboard. She had briefed us on Preston's group. They could be summarized as a typical skeleton film crew plus one lawyer, Sasha Sable.

As I mentioned, Preston does his own direction and putters in production, storyline, photography, casting, site selection and scenic design, costuming, stunt development, music, sound, dubbing and just about everything else that goes into creating a motion picture. A Preston Pavel Polar Production is just that. We found out there were to be two versions – one in Russian and one in English. There may be German, Chinese, Spanish, Italian, Arabic, Japanese, French and Nordic aftermarket varieties with subtitles. *(I wondered how Bruce Wallaroo would react to a Strine version.)*

Anyway, we were introduced to the group: the producer, Gustav Schäferhund; the female Panda cinematographer, Jane Huang Hau; the screenwriter Racoon Brothers; and the two assistants, Grizzly Bears Ella and Doris; as well as his lawyer, Sasha Sable who had arrived separately.

We introduced our team including Wolford on Skype. We did not mention Ursula 9 although Preston was aware of the AGI from his previous visit. She was running silently on a large laptop next to me.

Preston looked around the table and at the screen projecting Wolford, cleared his throat in an impressive rumble *(not as impressive as Octavius)* and said, "Well, now that we all know who is who, let us get right to the subject at hand. Bearoness and Doctor Bear, I envision this castle and its surroundings as being the ultimate location for the crowning achievement of my cinematic career. *(a little flowery but I think we all got what he meant.)* I want to take full advantage of the sea, the windswept cliffs, the forests and braes and of course, the castle itself. We will have to make adjustments in order to restore the buildings to their original ancient condition."

This last comment produced a gale of laughter from our team. Belinda giggled, "Forgive us, Preston, but this "ancient" castle began its life as a theme park about sixty years ago. Using the best research available, the old Bearon faithfully reproduced the character of a Scottish laird's residence. It was great commercial success. However, it wasn't until two generations ago that it was actually used by the late Bearon's relatives as an estate. On their recent departure, I began restoration to its theme park/resort/hotel status which is just about complete. Now, if we can reach financial and operational terms, Doctor Bear and I are willing to sustain some minor temporary cosmetic changes. I am sure that your famous and highly-skilled cinematographer, Ms. Hau, will be able to work around many of the more permanent facets of the building such as the air conditioning towers, heliport and parking facilities. I assume much of the interior work will be done in a studio far from here. I'm certain Herr Schäferhund has dealt with situations far more difficult than this. And of course, there is the sea, the wind-blown cliffs, the forest and the braes that are as nature intends them to be."

The Polar screen star grinned. "You are correct, Bearoness. Although I have no desire to do so, I could have our scenic designers reproduce this castle in true medieval form. But that would be a colossal waste of money. With careful scenic adjustments, script modifications and concentration on the natural environment, we can still produce a blockbuster. First, we must develop a scenario that allows me to show my millions of fans that Preston Pavel Polar is at the peak of his performing skills. We will require a supporting cast that will enhance my image. I was fascinated by your proposal that we use gangster cats as villains. *(See Book Eight-The Crank Case)* Are they available?"

I popped up. "I'm sure they can be, Preston but we also need to know the time and circumstances of their performance. Thirties? Roaring Twenties? Today or the "ancient" Scottish times? I have a thought that may allow you to make more extensive use of the castle as it is without much alteration."

"How about a period film within a more contemporary film? Imagine that you're the producer/director of a Preston Polar swordplay spectacular being shot here at Polar Paradise Resort *(name changed but nothing much else.)* In the external film surrounding it, you can use the pool and the Aquabears and Otto. Imagine you, Brittany and the rest of the cast outfitted with 1950's tuxedos, film director jodhpurs, slinky vamp gowns. Imagine a convertible limousine or two parked in front of the drawbridge. Imagine using the Village of Unst and the Lion and Unicorn pub for comic relief. Imagine still using the sea, cliffs, forests and braes as scenic background but not having to worry too much about the present-day character of the castle. Imagine me shutting up and letting you and your team do what you do."

"Oh no, Maury! Those are wonderful ideas. I like it. It gets me partially out of my usual swashbuckling image that I admit is getting stale but still lets me do what I do best. Still plenty of room for fights and stunts galore but updated. What do you think, Gustav, Jane, Racoons, Ella and Doris?"

Before any of them could utter a word, Preston slammed his paw on the table and said, "Good! I'm glad we all agree. Let's start work. Bearoness, I think we'll have to be resident here for at least three months. Maybe a little less. Can you have Mr. Wolverine join Sasha Sable and start drawing up contracts. Maury, can you contact the Feline Felons? By the way, what's the weather like here in late February, March and April. I don't want to hold up production."

Belinda smiled and said, "I think we can provide you with a storm or two, crashing breakers, howling wind and some snow, if that's what you want. Daylight will be in short supply for much of that period. April gets better. We actually get some sunshine along with fog and rain."

The matinee idol smiled his devastating smile. "That will all add to the dramatic effects. I have a very good feeling about this location. We'll have to be careful that it doesn't overwhelm us.

Chita

Chapter Six

Now a very short time has just passed
But the movie has fleshed out its cast
With production teams, too.
Bearyl makes her debut.
And the pace picks up speed very fast.

(Three weeks later!)

Semi-controlled chaos reigns supreme. Contracts have been signed. Scenarios are being furiously developed. Dialog is being written, scrapped and re-written by the Racoon Brothers. Actors and support staff are being signed up. The producer, Gustav Schäferhund is barking orders at everyone. Equipment is being shipped in. Ella and Doris have been down to Baltasound/Unst several times and have succeeded in reining in almost the entire population to play as extras in "The Laughing Laird", a fragmentary 17th century film within a film. The parent story will be set in the 1950's and will feature Preston as the Producer-Director Barton Bear in his castle retreat. He is under siege by a rival movie studio kingpin who wants to put him out of business.

The present-day castle complete with an Aquabear-filled swimming pool will be featured to illustrate Barton Bear's lifestyle. Current title: "The Pipes are Calling." When I foolishly pointed out that this phrase comes from an Irish ballad called "Danny Bear", I was told it didn't matter. Russian Bears think all Celts are the same and nobody else will care. Ah, Show Biz!

The "Laughing Laird" will be a short period piece *(or pieces)* designed to let Preston swash his buckles in his unique style of derring-do. Swordplay, bravado, incredible leaps, rescued damsels. *(Brittany)* "My fans will demand it." Much of it will be shot later in a Russian studio but supplemented with footage from previous epics plus the Shetlands scenic magic being collected right now.

Through all this, the resort hotel, Polar Paradise, still maintains its hospitable aplomb courtesy of Dougal, Phoebe Fairbearn and chef extraordinaire, Mrs. McRadish. In fact, when the press releases came out that the fabulous Preston Pavel Polar would be filming on site, reservations sky-rocketed. Polars and other animals from the four corners of the universe descended on the resort and took up positions to sightsee and hopefully land a small part as an extra. The bookings are actually exceeding our hefty holiday traffic.

Each morning, the sounds of helicopters and drones announce that Cinematographer Jane Huang Hau and her team are out gathering up background scenery and atmosphere. The castle is providing some hyper-ambiance for both films as are the sea, cliffs, forests and braes with a little snow and storms thrown in to round things out. Unst and the Lion and Unicorn pub are getting special handling. We also contracted for Jane to produce a short publicity clip for our resort.

I have arranged a return appearance of the fabulous Chita. She, along with her on-and-off musical associate, Jake the Jaguar will be touching down shortly much to the delight of Arabella and McTavish, the twin Octavian Cubs. Coming in separately will be another set of twins, Bearyl and Bearnice Blanc, Polar actress and singer respectively, and Bearnice's vocal partner, Leperello, *(Lepi)* the Himalayan Snow Leopard. Together, Chita, Lepi and Jake made up the original Feline Felons gang that so entertained Preston over the holidays. We were able to get our other feline brother and sister act, Benedict and Galatea Tigris, the very rare white Flying Tigers who pilot Octavius and Belinda's aircraft, to join in and add a growl or two during the fight scenes.

All told, progress is being made with the exception of a few glitches and the usual round of hissy fits. The budget, jointly bankrolled by Preston and the Octavians, has not been fiercely abused as yet.

Brittany has been playing Miss Temperamental. Not getting enough attention or as many lines to speak as she'd like. She is not enthralled by the arrival of Bearyl and Bearnice Blanc who could give her a run in the "Ingenue Polar" department. She also doesn't like her costumes. Sigh!

Several parts have been cast. Bearyl, an accomplished actress, will be playing the part of Barton Bear's studio chief, Bearnadette. Her sister, Bearnice will sing during an Aquabear pool spectacular featuring Belinda with comic relief by Otto. It's inserted in "The Pipes are Calling" to produce a fantasy flavor. It doesn't advance the plot an inch, but it does add to the opulent aura of the whole affair. *(See 1930's musical comedies.)*

The Feline Felons: Chita, Jake, Ben, Gal and Lepi have been getting into the lawless spirit of things with a vengeance. Lepi is playing the lead heavy and with his beautiful pelt and fabulous tail is bound to challenge the male Polars in the cast for OMG sex appeal. Not sure how Preston will feel about that. Of course, the gang gets it comeuppance *(that word again)* in the final reel.

Chita has mastered the trashy "moll" character and uses her long legs to sublime advantage. There's some debate about whether she should appear as her spotted self or her Black Panther alter ego. They've made a series of test shots and she's dynamite either way. Given her still outstanding record with various police forces, the Panther played by Ms. Catherine Catt would provide better cover. This isn't sitting too well with Brittany who wants to be the only female center of attraction.

The Cubs are making pests of themselves as only they know how. Mlle Woof will have her paws full, but I am certain that somehow, they will make a cameo appearance in the upcoming extravaganza.

Now comes the fascinating part. Belinda, Preston, Chita and I are all trying to persuade Octavius to play the part of the nasty, overpowering studio head who is set on getting Barton Bear *(Preston)* out of the movie business. You have to admit that a nine-foot Kodiak covered in dark brown fur and sporting a threatening frown and scary set of teeth would be a perfect contrast to the Polar hero. The Great Bear quite adequately played the part of Poppa Bear in our Goldilocks-based Christmas pantomime. At the moment, his interest in the film is restricted to the financing and resort-related logistics of the process. I have the greatest confidence in the Bearoness' ability to persuade him to step up to "Lights, Camera, Action." We shall see.

Chapter Seven

Things were going too smoothly, you see.
A dead Polar is fished from the sea.
She fell down from above
From a slip, push or shove.
We are wondering who she can be.

It had to happen! You really didn't think we could get this far without a major catastrophe, did you? Here's how it played out. Harold, the Sea Otter who is in charge of the Polar Paradise beaches, pools, sea craft and water sports was making his rounds in his outboard early in the morning when he came upon a Polar body floating in and out with the waves. Moments earlier, one of the cinematographer's drones, out for another round of seascape atmosphere, had captured a white object falling into the sea. But the film crew had not yet reviewed the drone's footage and wouldn't for a while.

When the Otter's call reached the hotel's security control center, several of the staff were immediately dispatched to the scene and dragged the very dead body back to the shore. Since the population of Polars at the hotel was large, it wasn't immediately clear who the victim was or how she *(it was a female)* had succumbed.

The security team called Dougal who in turn contacted the Unst constabulary. He then called Octavius and Belinda. Ms. Fairbearn and her staff were asked to check all the rooms that housed a female Polar, including the Aquabears, Bearyl and Bearnice, a number of guests and the film crew. Meanwhile, the body was left covered on the shore, awaiting the arrival of the police and coroner. Octavius and I went out to the site and without disturbing the body, looked for any unique signs that may have helped to identify the victim.

"She looks familiar," I said, "young and was once quite attractive."

"It could be any one of our guests. We're trying to narrow it down. Housekeeping is checking for anyone who seems to be missing from their rooms, but they could have just gone down for breakfast. I think the victim is too young to be one of the Aquabears and it's certainly not Bearyl or Bearnice," the Great Bear replied.

Suddenly it dawned on both of us. Octavius took out his phone. "Give me Mr. Preston Polar's room. Preston? Octavius Bear, we have a dead female Polar out here on the shore. Looks like she fell from the cliffs. I'm sorry, but Maury and I think it's Brittany. I'll have one of our security team bring you down here. Perhaps you can help us confirm the identification. No, we don't know what happened. Harold, our Sea Otter in charge of the beaches, found the body floating in the water while he was making his rounds. We've notified the police and the coroner. Thanks. We'll be waiting for you."

He turned to me. "Preston seems pretty shook up. I'm not sure what their relationship really was but at a minimum, assuming it's her, she was his 'ingenue du jour' for this film."

He called Belinda. "We're not certain but we believe the victim may be Brittany. Check around and find out if anyone has seen her this morning."

I looked at the corpse again and said, "Whoever it is, her body is pretty badly beaten up. She may have fallen off the cliffs. I know it cuts into the scenic charm of the place, but we really need to think about putting up wire fences, especially with the number of youngsters who play out there."

Octavius nodded his head in agreement. He looked up and said, "Assuming the tide hasn't moved it much, the trajectory of the body suggests she fell from the roof of the castle, not the cliffs."

"How would she get up there? The doors and the lifts are usually locked."

"The film crews have been installing equipment on the roof. They may have left the doors and the elevators unlocked. Wait, here comes Preston."

The film star came slowly trudging on all fours along with one of the security staff. He looked at us and then at the shrouded body. "Can you uncover it?" We did.

"That's her! She's wearing the necklace I gave her. Her face is all beaten but that's her."

He turned away and stared out over the ocean. "What happened? How did she get there?"

I replied, "We don't know. We think she fell from the roof of the castle."

"What the hell would she be doing up there?"

Octavius looked at him. "We don't know that, either. Was there any film-related reason for her to be on the roof?"

"Several of our stunts were scripted for the rooftop but none of them involved her. She was afraid of heights. Our stunt doubles had to cover for her whenever the script called for her to be threatened with falling."

"Who are the stunt doubles now that Paul and Paula have disappeared?'

"We haven't signed anyone yet. Tryouts are today and tomorrow."

"You're sure this is Brittany and not one of the stunt hopefuls?"

"No. it's her, alright." He shook his head, turned and lumbered back toward the hotel.

I thought I heard him say, "Stupid sow! We need to find a replacement quick!"

So much for sentiment.

*****

A short time later, the Unst Police Sergeant and the Coroner arrived on the scene by boat. The policeman, a Red Deer named Sergeant Alistair and Doctor Barclay, a Badger, took charge of the body.

While the Coroner examined the remains, the Sergeant took out his notepad and began his interviews.

"Who is she?"

Octavius, who was known to the Sergeant, replied. "We are reasonably certain her name is Brittany. We don't know her surname. She was an actress with the Preston Pavel Polar Productions group. They're shooting a movie here at Polar Paradise."

"Thank you, Doctor Bear. Who found the body?"

Harold the Otter responded. "I guess I did. I'm in charge of the water activities here at the hotel and I was making my morning rounds in my outboard looking for anything in the water that could endanger the guests. I saw the corpse floating near the shore."

The Sergeant said, "I'm going to put in a call to Shetland Yard. This is obviously a suspicious death. We're going to close off this section of the shore. Do you have any idea where she fell from?"

Octavius looked up at the castle and said, "We think she fell from the roof of the hotel. If she had fallen from the cliffs her body would have had to travel a long distance horizontally. Of course, she could have floated over this way. What do you think, Harold?"

"Och, Doctor Bear. I doubt it. The tides don't work that way."

The Sergeant closed his notebook and said, "We need to see the roof. I'm going to close it off until Shetland Yard makes its examination."

I piped up, "The film company has a lot of equipment up there along with technicians and other members of the company coming and going."

"Well, I'm sorry to discommode them but until we can prove it was an accident or suicide, I have to treat it as a crime scene. If she dropped from somewhere else, we'll have to examine that. I assume she had a room here. Did it face out over the water? Could she have gone out a window?"

None of us knew. The Great Bear frowned. "Maury, call Dougal!"

The Sheepdog responded immediately, "Aye, Mr. Maury. What can I do fer ye?"

"Dougal, where is Ms. Brittany's room?"

"It's actually a suite, sir. It's on the top floor with an ocean view. Right next to Mr. Preston Polar. I checked with Ms. Fairbearn. Ms. Brittany is not in her room."

"That figures. We think she's the corpse we fished out of the water. Do the windows in those suites open?"

"Aye, there's a balcony on each of those sixth-floor suites. It has a guard rail, of course, but ye can climb over it."

"OK, seal that room. The Police are going to want to go over it. Don't let housekeeping or anyone else get in there."

"Aye, sir. I'll have Ms. Fairbearn lock it up."

I turned to the Sergeant. "If it is Brittany, as we believe, her suite has an open-air balcony that looks out over the water. I think it's more likely she fell from there than the roof. I've had the room sealed."

"Thank you, Mr. Maury. I've just spoken to Superintendent Wardlaw. He and Mr. Fetlock Holmes are flying up here from Abeardeen on a Shetland Yard helicopter. They should be here in less than two hours. Meanwhile, the Coroner is examining the body. The fall probably killed her. There is no sign of drowning although that still needs to be proven."

Just as he said that, a Police launch drew up heading for one of the docks. Several uniformed policemen jumped out and came over to join the Sergeant. He started giving them orders to seal off the roof and the immediate shoreline.

Before they could set up the cordons, the film's Producer, Herr Gustav Schäferhund, *(known as a German Shepherd in the U.S. and Alsatian here in the British Isles)* came bounding over the rocky beach with the two assistants, Grizzly Bears Ella and Doris galumphing along behind.

"Herr Octavius, vot is this? Preston just told me that Brittany is "tot und begraben sein.""

"I'm sorry Herr Gustav. My German is not that good. If you mean she is dead in the water, you are correct. We haven't established for certain that it's Brittany, but we are reasonably sure.

"Mein Gott, how did this happen?"

"We don't know. She obviously fell but we're unsure whether she slipped, jumped or was pushed."

"Pushed? Do you think someone killed her?"

"It's just one possibility. We're not even sure where she fell from. Her suite has a balcony looking over the ocean, but she may also have been on the roof. Is any of your crew up there at the moment?"

He turned to the assistants. "Doris, Ella! Is anyone on the roof?"

I looked at the two bears and said, "If there is, tell them to stay there till the police come up."

Doris nodded her head, took out her phone and called one of the technical production crew. She looked back at the Sergeant, Octavius and me and said, "Jane Huang Hau and two of her staff are up there flying a drone, taking in the cliffs and the ocean for background scenery. I'll call her and pass on the news of the death and your request not to leave."

The Sergeant turned to the Producer. "We are going to want to see that drone's footage. It's possible it may have picked up her fall."

The Shepherd nodded his head. "Doris, tell Jane to hold on to this morning's shoot. The police will want to see it."

The Red Deer looked at Octavius and me and asked, "How do we get to the roof?"

"C'mon. I'll show you." I volunteered.

The Producer turned to the Great Bear and said, "Preston wants a replacement for Brittany as soon as possible. We don't have time in our production schedule for auditioning that role. He wants Fraulein Bearyl Blanc to step in. She was booked to play Barton Bear's studio chief, Bearnadette. Do you think the Bearoness could take on that character? It calls for a mature sow. Or perhaps we could alter or drop the part altogether. We do have to replace Brittany as Preston's sweetheart, however."

"You should talk to Bearyl about it. Maury is her agent. I'll chat with Belinda. I think she'd like to be the studio chief as long as she and the Aquabears can still do their act. Not too much sorrow being shown over Brittany's death, is there?"

"Frankly, Doctor Bear, I never cared for her. She was Preston's latest protégé. Beautiful but very high maintenance and not all that talented or competent. Of course, I certainly would not have wished this death on her, but I can't help feeling the film will be better off, especially with Fraulein Bearyl playing the part. I understand she has been touring as Lady Macbearth."

"Very successfully!"

"Ach, übrigens, can we interest you in playing the rival studio head? With your height, girth and dark fur, you'd be a wunderbar contrast to Preston. Don't worry, you don't get killed or roughed up. Just frustrated when you don't get your way. A few titanic roars and fierce looks which I understand you are quite capable of."

"Let me think about it. Do you have any options for our cubs? They are truly stage-struck."

"I think we'll use them in the Aquabear fantasy. They can cavort with Herr Otto."

Chapter Eight

Who's our very dead, young Polar sow?
Well, we know it's Ms. Brittany now.
Did she fall from the roof?
We could use some more proof
From the Cinematographer Hau.

(Up on the castle's roof.) Sergeant Alistair, two constables and I approached the Panda cinematographer and her crew. They had just finished landing their drone after its scenic tour.

"Good morning, Gentlebeasts. I'm Jane Huang Hau. Those two ferrets, Freddy and Frank, are part of my camera crew. I understand that Brittany took a fatal fall into the ocean."

"Yes, Ms. Hau. We think she may have fallen off the roof here. We're not sure when it happened."

"Well, she wasn't up here while we were working. We've been here since 8 AM. Did I understand that you want to review the footage taken by the drone this morning? It's primarily ocean and cliffs. We're going to use it as background for several of the stunts. There are also some shots of the castle. We're trying to get around the modernized aspects and show the building in a more traditional setting. If Brittany did fall from this rooftop, she would have had to climb over a five-foot wall or crawl up on one of the parapets. Pretty difficult."

I replied, "Over a year ago, one of the Bearoness' relatives was thrown over the wall into the moat. That was a nasty event. *(See Book 3 - The Case of Scotch)* He was slugged and then dragged unconscious and dumped. We caught the murderer, but it was pretty ugly. The same thing could have happened to Brittany. It doesn't seem as if she had been alone up here. You realize of course, that if she was pushed over the wall, you and your crew will be prime suspects."

The Giant Panda didn't like that one bit and said so. Her two crewmen put down the drone and came over to join her. "What's up, Jane?"

The Sergeant answered first. "We're investigating the death of Ms. Brittany. She was found in the ocean and was no doubt, killed by a fall from this building."

"Wow! Brittany's dead? That's going to put a crimp in the film. *(More sympathy for the dead Polar.)* Was it an accident, suicide or was she pushed?" This from Freddy who was wearing a Preston Polar jacket.

"We don't know yet. That's why we want to inspect the footage you took this morning with the drone. There may be something in there that might answer that question. I understand you took some shots of this building as well as the sea and surrounding scenery."

Frank nodded, "OK, we'll run you off a copy."

"No, we're going to need the original. You can keep a copy, but we want to make sure nothing has been changed or tampered with."

The Panda was again put out but agreed. "We'll want the original back."

"If there's nothing of value on it, you'll get it back soonest. If it turns out to be useful evidence, I'm afraid we'll have to impound it. We have a Superintendent from Shetland Yard and a famous consulting detective flying up as we speak. They'll want to inspect all the sequences. How many are there?"

"What have we got, Freddy?"

"About half an hour continuous. From 8:30 to 8:56! Here's the shot list."

"OK, as soon as the Super arrives, we'll have you set up a showing."

*****

A large utility chopper settled in on the Polar Paradise helipad. As the huge rotors slowly came to a halt, Octavius shambled over to the cargo access hatch and waved his equally huge paw. The stair-door opened, and a bearded collie stepped forward followed by a large black horse – Superintendent Nigel Wardlaw of Shetland Yard and the celebrated consulting detective, Fetlock Holmes.

"Welcome, gentlebeasts! I'm afraid Polar Paradise is becoming a possible crime scene once again. We have a film crew here shooting a swashbuckling pot boiler. I think you met Preston Pavel Polar over the holidays. He's making another one of his 'heart-stopping,' stunts and swords spectaculars here at the castle. Unfortunately, his principal ingenue polar sow, Brittany, *(no surname)* was found floating face down in the ocean this morning, quite dead. The Coroner has examined her body and says she died of impact, not drowning. Sergeant Alistair is here with several constables. Right now, they are up on the roof with one of the film crews. They had been shooting background scenery with a drone. There may be something in that footage that can tell us what happened."

"Where did she fall from?"

"We're not sure but we believe it was from the building, not the cliffs. She may have gone off the roof or the balcony of her suite. It faces the water."

Just then, a high-speed procession burst out of the castle drawbridge. The Cubs followed breathlessly by their Bichon governess, Mlle Woof and in more stately fashion the Bearoness herself.

"Hi Superintendent! Hi Mr. Houses! Remember us – Arabella and McTavish!"

Belinda pinched McTavish. "He's Mr. Holmes, not Mr. Houses."

The Horse snorted and said, "Good day, young Bears, I am glad to see you again."

Arabella twisted her mittens and looked at the detective. "Why are you here? Poppa, did something bad happen?"

"Yes, Bella. There's been an accident. Ms. Brittany fell into the ocean."

McTavish opened his eyes wide and asked, "Did she get hurt, Poppa?"

"I'm afraid she's dead, son.

"Oh, wow!"

The Cubs had been exposed to death several times in their young lives and understood the finality involved. Arabella looked at Belinda and said, "How did she fall, Momma?"

"We don't know yet, dear. That's why the Police are here. They want to know what happened, too.

Bella looked up at Fetlock Holmes. "Do you think somebody pushed her?"

Mlle Woof intervened. "Ma petite, we do not know. Why don't we let the police and Monsieur Holmes do what they are expert at?"

The Horse whickered. "Perhaps when you get a bit bigger, little Miss, you will become a great detective like your father."

McTavish shouted. "We both will."

Belinda laughed. "Now let's see. So far, you are going to be astronauts, archeologists, actors, basketball players and detectives. And that's only in the last six months. How about if you both grow up a bit more and Mlle Woof continues to polish up your education. Then you can work on careers."

"Can we be in Mr. Preston's movie?"

"We'll see." *(She thought, 'Not sure if there's going to be a movie.')*

The Coroner came over and shook paws and hooves with the Super and Holmes. "The impact killed her. The water is pretty shallow here. She hit face down. She may have hit bottom although water can be like cement if you drop from a significant enough height."

"Any signs of a struggle?"

"It's difficult to say. There are bruises on her back. The side that didn't hit the water. I'm not sure how they got there. I doubt if they were caused by the fall, but she may have been struck and then pushed."

"Let's get up to her suite and examine it. My money is on the balcony as her launch site."

Chapter Nine

Just one hour has swiftly gone past
And they're making a switch in the cast.
Seems Ms. Bearyl is now
The new ingenue sow.
Let us hope that this change is the last.

Preston Pavel Polar, Gustav Schäferhund, Doris and Ella were taking a quick strategy meeting. "I want Bearyl Blanc to replace Brittany, Gustav. Get with that Meerkat agent of hers and let's get going. Talk to the Bearoness. Offer her the part of Bearnadette, the studio chief. That calls for a mature sow. I suppose the Meerkat is her agent, too. Promise her we'll feature the Aquabears and that nutty Otter in the show sequence. Can you fit her two little brats in somewhere? See if you can interest Octavius in being the rival studio heavy and let's sign up those Cats to play the feline felons. They are a real sketch."

"I'm way ahead of you, Preston. I've had a conversation about all of that with Doctor Bear. I think he'll go along with it. If he does, convincing the Meerkat, the Ladies and the Cats should be easy."

"We need to get this thing back on track. How are the scripts coming? Tell the Racoon Brothers I'll want to have a session as soon as we finish here. What's with Jane and her film crew?"

"The Giant Panda has been shooting background material with a drone. This place is a scenic designer's dream."

"Well, let's not go too wild with the atmosphere. Remember who's the star of this show. Playing two parts is a first for me but I know my fans will love it. There are too many potential scene stealers in this cast, including this resort. Let's use them but this is still another Preston Polar spectacular. By the way, have we made any progress in getting the Bearoness and the Bear to invest in the production?"

"Their Wolverine lawyer and Sasha Sable are negotiating as we speak. After all, we're not paying for much of the Polar Paradise overhead."

"I know, but the processing and distribution costs are going to be heavy."

"By the way, what happens to Brittany's body? Does she have any next of kin?"

Preston frowned, "Not that I know of. Doris or Ella, you check on it. We'll probably have to wait for the Police to complete their investigation before they'll turn over the corpse. Damn it. I'll probably get stuck for her funeral and burial expenses. Stupid Sow!"

"I'll get the Racoon Brothers in here. We need to get the scripts locked down. This film within a film could get complicated."

"But it gives me a chance to play the hero twice in one show. That Meerkat is smart."

*****

Speaking of whom, I am back from my sojourn on the roof. I had left the Sergeant with the film crew who were making a copy of the drone's morning meanderings. As I left the elevator *(lift)* in the Main Hall, I ran into Dougal and Phoebe Fairbearn. The Chief Housekeeper asked if there was anything she or her staff could do to assist in the investigation.

"1 don't know, Phoebe. *(We are on a first name basis.)* Octavius, Detective Holmes and the Police Superintendent have gone up to Brittany's suite. You can keep the maids and other staff out of the rooms until they have completed their review." I turned to Dougal. "I don't think she fell off the roof, she would have had to crawl over the wall or one of the parapets."

"Are ye sure she fell, Mr. Maury? Could she not have committed suicide?"

"Good question, Dougal, and I don't have a good answer."

The Housekeeper ran off to ensure the staff stayed out of Brittany's suite. Dougal went out to the courtyard to see if the helicopter crew needed anything and I turned around and stared into the cold black nose of Gustav Schäferhund who had just exited the elevator."

"Ah, Herr Meerkat, just the animal I want to see."

"Call me Maury!"

"Ja, Maury, and I am Gus! As you know, we have lost Brittany as our ingenue. I have spoken to Doktor Bear about having Fraulein Bearyl take the part. He referred me to you as her agent. He also suggested that I speak to you about the Bearoness playing the part of the Studio Chief, Bearnadette. That was the part Fraulein Bearyl was going to play. However, she is still young, not quite an ingenue but young nevertheless and quite attractive, experienced and should fit the role of Bearbara quite nicely."

"Bearbara?"

"Ja, that is the ingenue's name. Brittany didn't like it. She wanted to use her own name."

"And the Bearoness as Bearnadette, the Studio Chief?"

"That really calls for a more mature sow and the beautiful Bearoness fits it to a B. Ach, übrigens, Doktor Bear would make a fantastich rival studio head. He's the original, how do you say, 'heavy'."

"Well, I don't represent Doctor Bear, but I am his sidekick, er, associate. I think I can talk him into it provided he doesn't have to do anything criminal or ridiculous. He played the part of Poppa Bear in our Christmas pantomime which was ridiculous enough."

"Nein, all he has to do is lose his temper."

"He's good at that. I also represent the Five Feline Felons. I'll talk to all of them. Meanwhile, why don't you have Sasha Sable draw up your usual contracts and we'll get moving. Let me know if you are going to want to sign any of our staff as extras."

"Ja, I understand Doctor Bear has two wolves on his staff."

"Yes, Frau Ilse Schuylkill. A beautiful European grey wolf. She's Octavius' Swiss estate manager/cook/pilot/security officer with many other mysterious and military talents like sharpshooting. And Wyatt Where. An American red wolf. He's Frau Schuylkill's mate and a former military intelligence officer who retired to a security post at a bank in Chicago and then quit to join Octavius. They are both formidable animals. They both practice *Höchstgeschwindigkeit* - hyperspeed movement. Now you see them, now you don't. The Frau is a master at it. However, I doubt you could convince them to take parts in the film, but you can try."

"I should like to meet them anyway. We schäferhunds have much in common with wolves, especially the greys. Does the Frau speak German?"

"I don't think so. She speaks English, of course and Switzerdeutsch which she informed me once is definitely NOT German."

"Ah well, We'll struggle through. Could you arrange for us to have drinks together later today?"

"Sure, how about five in the Main Hall lounge. I'll be able to give you an update on your other prospective actors, as well. Right now, I want to find out what is happening with our mystery death."

"Perhaps you could also let me know as well. I suppose it's too early for theories."

"I think so. I'll let you know what I know when we get together."

Off I went in search of the Great Bear and his law enforcement associates, Superintendent Wardlaw and Fetlock Holmes. They were either in Brittany's suite or up on the roof with the camera crew.

Frau Schuylkill

Chapter Ten

Did Ms. Brittany fall on her own?
Was she pushed, shoved or possibly thrown?
We are eager to see
What the answer might be
With some help from the films on the drone.

I found them in what had been Brittany's sixth floor suite – a sitting room, bath and bedroom. A balcony ran the length of the suite. Sliding doors in each room gave access to the platform. Both were open. Octavius was standing out there on all fours, examining the railing that stood about five feet high. Part of it was bent outward. Inside, Holmes was scanning the floor for pawprints and other indicia. The Superintendent was searching the drawers and closets. Phoebe Fairbearn was standing by the door.

The horse whinnied and said, "Gentlebeasts, Miss Brittany had company here sometime in the hours since the maids last vacuumed the rug. There are two sets of bear paw indentations of differing sizes here. Nothing but some dust under the chairs, table and bed."

Octavius reentered the suite and waved in my direction. "Hello Maury! It seems our ingenue made a rather violent exit from the room. She hit the guard rail with enough force to bend it slightly. I suspect she was thrown or pushed by an animal or two of some strength. I doubt if she went voluntarily. One of the sliding doors is off its track. She may have grabbed and pulled on it, trying to hold on. Anything of interest in the drawers or closets, Superintendent?"

"Not really. Some clothing, jewelry and a paper copy of what I guess is a preliminary film scenario. No correspondence. Oddly, there is no smart phone or laptop. I assume she had one or more. Whoever pushed or threw her probably took it with them. I think we can work on a preliminary assumption that she was killed by parties unknown for reasons yet unknown. I'll have the constables check the neighboring rooms to see if anyone heard or saw anything. Ms. Fairbearn, who are in the adjoining rooms?"

"The suite next door is Mr. Preston's. The producer has the room opposite and the cinematographer is two doors down. The other suites are empty for the moment, but they are reserved by guests unrelated to the filming."

Octavius said, "We believe Preston was in his room when we called him to come down and identify the body. Maury, did you or Dougal call him on the house phone or his smartphone?"

"I called on the house system. I don't have his smartphone number.

Fetlock Holmes asked, "Mr. Meerkat, do we have the film yet that the camera crew was taking with their drone?"

"They were making a duplicate and giving us the original. They are going to set it up for viewing in one of the conference rooms. I'll check and see if it's ready."

I called Jane Huang Hau. She and her team were in the John Bearymore Conference Room and were waiting on us. I passed on this information to the three detectives.

The Great Bear told Phoebe Fairbearn to keep the suite sealed as we headed down for the show. As usual, because of his size, weight and girth, Octavius took the freight elevator. This time he was joined by Holmes, no small animal himself. The Super and I took the more conventional lift.

When we arrived, the cinematographer waved us in and said, "There's some interesting stuff on here but we'll run the entire set for you. There may be something you see that we don't."

The first ten minutes were taken up with panoramic shots of the ocean, cliffs, shoreline, forest and sky punctuated by brooding clouds. Nice background material but nothing compelling or helpful to our cause. Then the camera shifted to the castle itself. It started out on the rooftop with shots of the crew and then retreated out over the water as it scanned the ocean side of the building, As it swept across the walls and windows on its way to the courtyard side, a brief flash of white intruded on the scan and then disappeared.

Octavius shouted, "Hold it right there! Back up! Is that what I think it is?"

The Panda replied, "That's what we wanted to show you, I think that's Brittany taking a dive."

I asked, "I don't suppose you have sound?"

"No, all you'd get is the noise from the drone's motors. We dub the sound and music in later at a studio."

"Can you give us slow motion?"

"Sure, we're shooting right below the balconies on the sixth floor. The drone and the white object are moving in different directions so you're not going to get a steady view but I'm willing to bet that's her falling. She's rotating."

"Which suggests she got shoved although it's not conclusive."

"Well," said the Horse, "with the other evidence we saw in the room, I think we have a case of murder on our hooves."

The Superintendent agreed, and Octavius uttered one of his trademark "Hmmms."

"Is there anything else worth looking at, Ms. Hau?"

"Not unless you're interested in castle architecture. There's nothing else of the ocean side of the building. We have some good shots of the drawbridge and the moat."

Chapter Eleven

We're expanding the shifts in the cast
And the changes are coming quite fast.
Agent Maury's on call
To take care of them all
And I'm feeling quite simply harassed.

I spent the rest of the afternoon tracking down the potential new cast members of this cinematic epic. Bearyl was happy to give up her role as the studio chief to play Brittany's part as the ingenue, Bearbara.

"I feel kinda' creepy replacing a dead actress, Maury, especially the way she died. You don't suppose the role had anything to do with her death?"

"I really doubt it, Bearyl. We're not sure who or what caused her fall, but she wasn't very popular."

"She threatened me the other night. She said I wanted her part. Me with my starring resumé on the stage. She thought I wanted to make it big in films, too. But she wasn't going to let that happen. She told me I'd better be careful."

"Oh boy, you'd better pass that on to Octavius. She didn't hit you or shove you, did she?"

"She wouldn't dare. She was half my size."

I scrunched up my nose. "But she sure had a nasty streak. Nobody liked her."

"Enough to get her killed?"

"No, I suppose not. Something serious happened though, but as of the moment, the great investigative craniums are being mutually scratched. They're not quite clueless but damn near."

"Well anyway. I'll take the part. Let's get the contract signed and let me have a copy of the script."

"The contract will be here shortly, but the script is still 'in development.'"

"Where have I heard that before!"

"Every time you're in a show. Even Shakesbeare gets modified. The Racoon Brothers are good, though. I think you'll like your part. Lot's of emoting!" *(I said that with my paws crossed.)*

Bearyl's twin, Bearnice is a dynamite singer and will be part of the Aquabear show.

Next stop, the Bearoness! She was more than willing to take on the studio chief's part. She was also going to lead the spectacular swimming number in the film within a film. She would negotiate the contracts for the Aquabears. They were Belinda's employees. I need to sign up Otto and his hi-jinks. She asked me how we could get the cubs a little show biz time. I told her it was on Herr Schäferhund's to-do list.

On to the Feline Felons – Chita; Jake the Jaguar; Lepi *(Leperello)* the Himalayan Snow Leopard; and Ben and Gal, The Flying Tigers. They've all been practicing menacing snarls and Chita was perfecting her floozy act. *(Not for the first time.)* They were on board. I hoped the lawyers had plenty of contracts available.

Now, the uphill climbs. Octavius and the Wolves. At first, Octavius waved off the idea claiming that helping to finance this escapade was a sufficient contribution. Belinda to the rescue! She told him what a riot he was as Poppa Bear in the Christmas pantomime. A natural actor. *(See Book Eight – The Crank Case)* He finally gave in. He doesn't need much rehearsal. Throwing a fit comes naturally.

I spoke briefly to the Wolves and convinced them to join Herr Schäferhund and me at five in the Main Lounge. Frau Schuylkill was very reluctant, but the Colonel talked her into it. "If nothing else, you can meet another German Shepherd."

"I was married to one and he turned out to be a schweinhund. This picture-making business is just a pile of silliness. It's almost as bad as those fashion shows. I am fond of Chita but there are times when I wonder about her and her media for females." *(See Book Nine – The Basket Case)*

Anyway, we shall see. I didn't think the Producer (or Preston, for that matter) had met L. Condor *(Condo)* so I invited him to join us as well. A big, black bird with a 12-foot wingspan and a technically augmented voice box, Condo is a consummate vocal mimic. He and Otto supply comic relief in a lot of circumstances. But both of them are serious and skilled when it comes to crime and detection. All told we have an impressive crew.

Speaking of impressive, we are past due communicating with Ursula 9, our Artificial Intelligence Unit. I got hold of Octavius, Super Wardlaw, and Fetlock Holmes and called up the AGI on a large screen monitor. Ursula had been with us on the shore when Brittany's body was recovered and later when we were inspecting her room. She was also on board while we were looking at the footage from the drone. She was in passive mode in each instance. We don't want to advertise her presence or capabilities to too many people. However, Preston Polar is aware of her, even if he doesn't understand who or what she is. *(See Book Eight – The Crank Case)*

"OK, Ursula, let's hear your thoughts on this mess."

"Certainly, Doctor Bear! I concur that this was no accident and all my probability algorithms strongly discourage suicide as a cause of death. Deliberately jumping was not consistent with her personality. That leaves murder by animal or animals unknown. She wasn't the largest polar bear by any means, but it would still take a strong individual to push her hard enough to bend the balcony safety rail. It could have been more than one creature but the footprints on the rug in her room suggest only two were involved – Brittany and her killer. At the moment, given the proximity of their suites, Brittany's continued complaints and clinging vine activities, and the strength required, my top candidate is Preston Pavel Polar. I hasten to add, we have insufficient evidence to make that case."

Holmes intervened, "I can see your point but don't forget losing his ingenue is setting back the film production. I'm sure that's his top priority."

I answered, "But that may be why he killed her. Now with Bearyl in the role, he has an experienced, attractive and highly skilled substitute. The crew can easily make up for lost time and expense. Perhaps that was his motive, if it is him. Get rid of the pesky, temperamental no-talent and put a true professional in her place."

Octavius grunted, "Let's not get ahead of ourselves here. We don't have anywhere near enough evidence to back up that accusation, regardless of what we believe. We need to keep an open mind, keep gathering data and look for other suspects."

Super Wardlaw concurred. "There is also the possibility that this was a spontaneous act brought on by Brittany's acerbic personality. She may have been making threats or even engaging in blackmail. A violent, impulsive response and over she goes."

Octavius agreed. "Let's open up our web here. There are other possibilities. I hate to say this, but we will have to thoroughly check out Bearyl. She has much to gain from Brittany's death."

I choked as I thought back to Bearyl's being threatened by Brittany. Not the right time to bring that up in front of Wardlaw and Holmes. "C'mon Octavius! Bearyl? You've got to be kidding. We've known and trusted her for years. She hasn't got a murderous bone in her body."

"You know that, and I know that. But she does have a temper. Remember Winnipeg? *(See Book Four – The Lower Case)* We have to make sure she's in the clear just like we did in Canada."

That didn't particularly satisfy me, but I guess I had to agree. I decided to keep my mouth shut for the nonce. I work for the Great Bear but I'm Bearyl's agent. I'm going to keep a tight grip on this one. It was getting on to five o'clock. Time for the Wolves, Condo and I to meet with Herr Schäferhund. Maury, the agent rides again.

Chapter Twelve

Schäferhund is entranced by the Frau
And he's willing to sign her right now.
But the she-wolf says no!
She's not willing to go.
She thinks film-making's much too low-brow.

Five PM. Herr Schäferhund, with Germanic precision and punctiliousness unusual in the movie business, arrived on the spot in the Main Lounge accompanied by Doris and Ella, his grizzly ursine assistants. Not to be outdone, the Wolves, Condo and I swept into the room, signaled Fiona to send over one of the wait-staff to take our orders, and joined in a round of mutual introductions.

The Producer was clearly taken with the Frau. Why not? She was beautiful, authoritative, highly intelligent, mysterious and supremely confident. The Colonel watched, partly amused. Did I detect a little jealousy there? Perhaps. After all, she was his mate.

Condo broke the ice with his vocal mimicry which sent Doris and Ella into spasms of laughter. Even the hound broke up. "Oh, Herr Condor, we must use you. Some will think it's a technical trick that we have dubbed but between your size, your unique face and your endless supply of voices, you will steal a good few minutes of laughter."

He looked at me. "Herr Meerkat, I didn't realize what a gold mine of talent we have here. I must inform the Racoon Brothers to meet with your people and fit them into the scripts."

The Frau reneged. "Herr Schäferhund, I am sorry but acting is not an appropriate occupation for a former military wolf. I believe the Colonel shares my opinion. Our primary roles when we are on site, away from our headquarters in Cincinnati, are protection and detection. We are concerned by the death of Fraulein Brittany. Was that a single event or the beginning of a series? Who is responsible? We have already been involved in several deaths and attacks here at the castle. This place seems to attract danger. We will be too busy helping to ensure the safety of all the parties concerned to be emoting in front of a camera. Danke!!"

The Colonel nodded in agreement.

"Well," said the Producer, "That is disappointing. I shall have to inform Preston that he will be without wolves in his extravaganza."

L. Condor looked the hound in the eye and said, "I am willing to participate in your cinematic sport but like my friends and cohorts here, my first obligation is to support Doctor Bear, the Bearoness, the Cubs and all of the rest of animals here including you, your staff and crew. I believe you'll find us all of one mind. For example, don't think that little Otto is strictly a clown. He has proven to be quite formidable when called upon. His special skills can be quite useful when difficulties arise. And Maury here is a first-class detective in addition to being Octavius' assistant and our theatrical agent. We're a flexible lot."

The Producer went off. He had an appointment with Preston. The Wolves and Condo also left. I asked Doris and Ella to stay on and join me in a drink. I said I wanted to get acquainted and coordinate our activities. I needed to learn a bit more about these two grizzlies. I wondered how well they got along with Brittany, if anyone got along with Brittany.

The two of them seemed quite impressed with our team, the castle and especially Octavius and Belinda. Ella gushed, "And those Cubs. They are just fabulous. So bright and active. And their wonderful coloration. So unique! I didn't know polars and Kodiaks could mate and have offspring. How old are they?"

"Just approaching three. It's rare for the two species to crossbreed but when they do, look out. Of course, their parents are both exceptional. Octavius is a super-genius and the Bearoness is no intellectual slouch, either. They are both independently hyper-wealthy and Belinda, as you can see, is stunningly beautiful. She is a terrific show-bear and manages this resort and the Aquabears. The Shetland Islanders love her. She is also a highly skilled helicopter and jet pilot. For a humble Kalahari Meerkat, I live in a rarefied atmosphere. But tell me about yourselves."

"Well," said Doris, "even though we're both grizzlies, we aren't related. As you can see, my coat is almost black while Ella is tan. I come from Alaska and Ella is from Wyoming. We met while applying for studio jobs in Hollywood. Both of us want to act but it's tough to break into films."

Ella picked up the tail. "Herr Schäferhund was making an epic in California and the call went out for a couple of PAs, sorry, production assistants. We got the jobs. We needed something that paid money. I typically take care of the office administration, script handling, hiring and firing and general logistics. For example, I'm scheduling try-outs for the new stunt doubles, and I liaise with the staff here at the castle."

Doris said, "I'm a set PA. I work the actual shooting events, scripts, scheduling, keeping track of the film, equipment, crew and actors. This is our third film with 'Herr Hund' as we call him. It's our first with Preston Polar. Not the easiest thing in the world."

"Why is that?" I asked.

"Personalities mostly. although some of the stunts and situations are hair-raising, too."

"I assume Preston is very demanding."

"Yeah, and so was Brittany. Speak well of the dead and all that, but she was a real bitch. Complaining, putting us down. Throwing it up to us that she had a real starring role while we were dime-a-dozen flunkies. Can't say I'm sorry she's gone. I understand Bearyl is a real sweetheart, by comparison."

"I've known Bearyl for quite some time. She's competent, intelligent, cooperative and not the least bit stuck up. You'll like her."

"Well, that's a relief. Brittany was making this shoot a real nightmare. How did you end up being an agent?"

"I've been Octavius' sidekick for quite a while and working with him is still my number one job. When we first met Otto, he was trying to make it as a magician. His career was not going well. But he was victimized by a truly nasty and insane duck, Imperius Drake, who promised to make him a star. He was actually using Otto as an experimental animal, altering his genes and trying to create a super creature that would be subject to his will. He failed, but not before Otto developed his ability to zap-teleport. Imperius is dead and Otto is now a star attraction with the Aquabears plus a daunting detective. He asked me to be his agent and I agreed. I've since taken on a few more clients, as you know."

Ella replied, "We've signed him and your whole team except the wolves. They all should really make a difference, especially the Feline Felons and the Aquabear Review. The Racoon Brothers are frantically updating the scripts to get them on board."

Doris snorted, "Preston is afraid they may upstage him. He's a walking ego. Thanks for the drinks. We've got to get back to work. Stunt double try-outs. First thing in the morning."

As they rumbled out, I picked up my smartphone and asked, "OK, Ursula, what's your take?"

"Both grizzlies are very definitely suspects, Maury. They are big enough to handle her and if Brittany was giving either one or both a hard time, she may have been given the heave-ho. They're certainly not crazy about Preston either, but he's their meal ticket for the moment."

"Speaking of meals, it will be dinner time in another hour or two. It's a shame you don't eat or drink."

"But I can smell food and the bouquet of a fine wine. It's very pleasant."

"I think it's time we got together again with the Great Bear, the Superintendent and the Consulting Detective and compared notes."

"Agreed! Before you do, you may want to speak with the Chief Housekeeper. It seems Brittany struck one of the maids. Ms. Fairbearn went to her room this morning and protested. I'm not sure she wanted you to know that fact given her recent scrape with the law about her son."

"Are you telling me we may have another possible culprit on our paws? How do you know about this?"

"Observation, my dear Mr. Meerkat, observation!"

"Let's go talk to the sleuths. I'll get with Phoebe later."

Chapter Thirteen

Phoebe Fairbearn arrives on the scene.
Seems Ms. Brittany acted quite mean
To the maid on her floor.
Chased her out through the door.
And the Housekeeper took out her spleen.

I managed to find the three investigators in a conference room where they were doing exactly what I wanted to do – comparing notes.

"Hello Maury! Come on in and join the discussion. How did your session with the Producer, the Wolves and Senhor Condor go?"

"Fine, Octavius! Condo is willing to play but the Wolves are not. They believe acting is inappropriate."

"I'm beginning to think so, too."

"Oh, don't you start. After all, you have an investment in this flick and your wife and cubs want you to do it. As do I. And you've signed a contract. Your part's a breeze. Just act natural. Have another tantrum."

A large Kodiak paw swished past my head.

"I have a few items I would like to stir into the pot. I had a session with the two PAs."

Holmes whickered, "PAs??"

"Production assistants. Doris and Ella. They couldn't stand Brittany and she took every opportunity she could to demean them both."

Super Wardlaw chuckled, "That Polar sow seems to have provided ample motive for murder to everyone she came in contact with. Do you know of any more specifics?"

"Not yet. I didn't want to press until I spoke with you. Ursula thinks they are definitely candidates for the Brittany Free Fall contest. Speaking of Ursula, who is right here with me as she is with you, she has unearthed an incident between Phoebe Fairbearn and Brittany that happened this morning. It seems the ingenue struck one of the maids and Ms. F. went to her room to protest."

Octavius sighed, *(a sound that triggers storm warnings)* "Motives, motives, motives! Maybe we should arrest the entire hotel and get it over with. Let's see. We have Preston Polar, Bearyl *(I winced.)* Doris, Ella, and Ms. Fairbearn. I don't think anyone else on our own team had anything to do with Brittany. The cinematographer and her crew were busy on the roof when Brittany took her dive. The script writers are a real long shot. What about the producer?"

"I suppose he's a possible. The film should go more smoothly since she's out of it."

Fetlock Holmes turned his noble head and said, "I think the time has come for us to do some in depth interviews. We can speculate forever. We are agreed, are we not, that Ms. Brittany was assisted in her trip over the handrail and that we are dealing with a murder?"

Affirmative nods all around.

"The prints we have on the rug of the suite look like bear prints. If true, that might eliminate Herr Schäferhund but everyone else on our list is ursine. We have plenty of motive and some cases of opportunity. We need to narrow that down further."

Superintendent Wardlaw growled. The Border Collie was clearly frustrated. "I assume we still have that suite sealed off."

Octavius nodded.

"I think we need to go over it again for additional evidence. Blood, for example. Is it possible Brittany scratched or wounded her assailant? Are any of our suspects sporting an injury?"

"Not that I've seen, but it's not difficult to hide a scratch under a bear's pelt. I haven't observed anyone limping or favoring a paw. By the way, tomorrow morning the tryouts for the stunt doubles begin. They're going to have to find a match for Bearyl instead of Brittany."

"How many candidates are there?"

Ursula interrupted. "Four males and three females. The males are all Preston's size. The females are a bit smaller than Bearyl. Brittany was somewhat diminutive. Ella brought them all on this afternoon in one of the Polar Paradise utility helicopters. They're checked in and are having dinner as we speak. One of the females is quite upset about Brittany's death. She believes it's bad luck."

Octavius grumped. "Well, it certainly was for Brittany. Are we going to have a 'this film company is cursed!' situation on our paws?"

"I doubt it. Preston and 'Herr Hund' won't put up with it."

"Herr Hund?"

"That's what the crew all call Herr Schäferhund. I'm not sure what they call Preston and I can't repeat what they called Brittany. Before we go to dinner, I think you, Belinda and I need to chat with Phoebe Fairbearn. We'll pass on the conversation to you, Superintendent and Mr. Holmes. Why don't you go off duty and have a drink? Are the constables still here?"

"Two still are. The others have taken the body down to the Abeardeen morgue."

"OK, Maury, call Belinda and Phoebe. Better get Dougal in on this too."

*****

Fifteen minutes later, castle management plus me sat down in the Winnie-the-Pooh conference room. Ursula was running in silent mode for the moment. Octavius let me lead off.

"Phoebe, we need to ask you a few questions about Brittany."

The Chief Housekeeper looked around the room quizzically and locked her vision onto Belinda. "I'm not sure what you mean, Mr. Meerkat."

"We understand you had a discussion with her this morning shortly before her death."

"Yes, I did. She had struck Angela, one of our housemaids, last night, accusing her of stealing a piece of jewelry. She was drunk. The bracelet turned up under her bed, but she insisted Angela hid it there. She tried to hit her again but missed and fell over. Angela ran from the suite and looked for me. When I came to her room, she had passed out. So Angela and I returned this morning and had it out with her. I told her in no uncertain terms that her behavior would not be tolerated and insisted that she apologize to Angela. She was obviously hung over and unwilling to listen or say she was sorry. She cursed at both of us."

"Did she attempt to strike either one of you?"

"No, she threw a glass bowl in our general direction and told us to get the hell out. We left and I called Dougal."

Dougal nodded and said, "Before I could get up there, she had taken her fall."

Belinda asked, "Angela was with you the whole time?"

"She was. Please talk with her. I intended to go back with Dougal, but events overtook us."

Octavius said, "I don't think I know Angela."

"She is a red deer, very competent and honest as can be. Brittany was definitely in the wrong."

"When we examined the suite, there were several sets of bear footprints but no deer hoofprints."

Dougal spoke up. "The maids wear soft slippers, Doctor Bear. That was one of the Bearoness' ideas."

Belinda agreed, "We don't want the domestic staff making unnecessary noise when they are working the floors. We even check that the rooms are empty before running the vacuums."

"No one has cleaned the rooms since Brittany's fall?"

"No! I was told to seal the room and I did immediately. Only the Police have been in there."

I asked, "When she threw the glass bowl, did it break?"

"I don't think so. I remember it bounced."

Octavius agreed. "There was a glass bowl on the rug. We assumed it had fallen over during a struggle. Probably not! Did she have a smartphone or laptop there?"

She pawsed for a moment. "I remember seeing a laptop on her night table. I don't remember seeing a phone."

"Any other questions for Ms. Fairbearn? No? OK, Phoebe. Thank you! Sorry you and Angela had to go through that. Please send Angela in to speak to us. That way we can tie the event up and get on with our investigation."

"Thank you all! I'll send Angela down. Please be gentle with her, She's still quite upset."

After she closed the door, Octavius snorted. "It would seem that whoever did Brittany in, took her laptop with them. Nothing else seems to be missing. There's something on that computer the killer wanted. We need to find it."

*****

A tentative knock on the conference room door. Belinda called out, "Come in, Angela." The maid, a frightened red deer, stepped in, hesitated and stopped at the end of the table. She looked around the room, recognizing Dougal and The Bearoness. She curtseyed and cast her eyes on Dougal.

"Angela, my lass. Don't be afraid. Come and sit down. No one is going to bite you. We just want to ask you a few questions about the trouble you had with Ms. Brittany."

"Oh, sair, I am still so upset. 'Twasn't my fault. She called me a thief and struck me. She was in her cups, alright. I could barely understand her. I didn't take her bracelet. 'Twas under the bed, it was. I'm a good girl. I wouldna steal from anyone, specially our guests."

Belinda smiled. "I'm sure that's true. We believe you. We just want to hear your version of your visit to her suite this morning with Ms. Fairbearn."

The deer briefly stared at each of us. Clearly, she was not sure what to make of Octavius. A nine-foot, 1400-pound Kodiak whose natural expression was a frown is enough to frighten anyone. A two-foot tall *(plus tail)* Meerkat, on the other hand, usually evokes laughter or at least a smile. The Bearoness had the power to take away or let her keep her job. She was uncomfortable in spades.

"Well, Milady, after I ran from Ms. Brittany's suite last night, I went to Ms. Fairbearn and told her my story. She was angry and stormed up to the sixth floor. We found Ms. Brittany snoring on her bed, out cold from too much drink. Ms. Fairbearn told me we would go back in the morning and face her down. Next day, she came for me and we went up to the suite."

Octavius asked, "What time was this?"

His rumbling voice did little to put the deer at ease. She thought for a moment. "About eight o'clock, sair. The mornin' shift was just comin' on. I was getting' ready to go home after we went back to Ms. Brittany's room."

I smiled and asked, "Was she awake?"

"Just bearly, sair. I'm sure she was hung over. Ms. Fairbearn told her off good and proper. She didn't pay any attention except to tell us both to go to Hell and then she threw a crystal drinks bowl at us. Ms. Fairbearn said she was going to call Mr. Dougal and have her tossed out of the hotel."

Dougal nodded his head and said, "By the time Phoebe reached me, Harold had reported her body was floatin' in the ocean."

The deer started to cry. "I'm sure that's not what Ms. Fairbearn meant by tossing her out."

Octavius smiled *(scary enough with all his teeth)*. "No, of course not! Did you see a laptop computer the last time you were in the suite this morning.?"

"Yes sir. It was on the night table."

"How about a smartphone?"

"No, I didn't see one."

I said, "You two may have been the last ones to see her alive."

Belinda looked over at me. "Except for whoever pushed her off the balcony."

That started Angela on another round of sobs. The Bearoness looked at her and said, "Go home, Angela. You live down in the village, don't you? If you don't feel up to coming into work this evening, call Ms. Fairbearn and tell her I said you could miss an evening."

"That is very kind, Milady but I'll be fine. You are all so wonderful. So is Ms. Fairbearn. The staff all love her."

After the deer had left, Belinda turned to Dougal and said, "I think our Chief Housekeeper's job is looking more and more secure."

Chapter Fourteen

The stunt double sinks down with a roar.
Preston Polar wants "just one jump more."
The bear gets up and he grunts.
He'd just done this fall once.
By tomorrow he's gonna be sore.

The production crew had taken over the main ballroom, the moat and the drawbridge of the castle. They had also set up on the side of one of the cliffs. A grouping of unfinished furnishings was laid out in the ballroom's interior including drapes and a stairway to nowhere. All this and more to conduct stunt double tryouts.

The seven candidate polar bears were split up into groups and assigned to the different locations. The males were being called on to do solo stunts and then "damsel in distress" rescues of the females. Preston was there to engage in swordplay and leaps. Each of the males had to "die" several times at the star's paws. Then they had to switch identities and emulate Preston's derring-do. Falling off the drawbridge; leaping off the drawbridge; falling into the moat; avoiding the moat while dueling; climbing the draperies; jumping from the stairs and so on and so on. All with nets and pads, of course. Doris and Ella had seen to that along with several stunt coordinators and special effects supervisors who had arrived along with the candidates.

The Cubs had begged Belinda and Ms. Woof to be allowed to watch from a safe distance. They were mesmerized. "Momma, was Ms. Brittany trying a stunt when she fell into the ocean?"

"I don't think so, dear. These people are all professionals trained in their specialties. Ms. Brittany was an actress. She wasn't allowed to do dangerous stunts."

"Well, how did she fall, Momma?"

"We don't know yet, Tavi. That's what Poppa, Uncle Maury, Superintendent Wardlaw and Mr. Holmes are trying to find out."

"Is Aunt Bearyl going to replace Ms. Brittany? She was fun as Momma Bear in the Christmas pantomime?"

"Yes, she is."

"Will she be doing stunts?"

"No, I won't," said a voice from behind them. "At least not the dangerous ones."

"Aunt Bearyl," squeaked Arabella, "This so cool. I love being with all of you actors and performers. Momma and the Aquabears and Otto are really great. And so were you and even Poppa and Uncle Maury in the pantomime. And the Lion King we saw in Noo Yuck was awesome. Tavi and I want to be actors."

Belinda laughed, "That's this week. Poor Mlle Woof has to deal with their latest crazes all the time. Astronauts, archaeologists, basketball players, actors!"

"Well," squeaked Tavi, "astronauts can be actors, too, you know. But I really want to be a famous detective like Poppa and Fetlock Holmes. I bet I could be a fabulous stunt bear, too. I could rescue you, Bella. I'd jump off a wall and take you away from the nasty guys who are trying to kidnap you and hold you for ransom to get Poppa and Momma's money."

"I've already done that. Uncle Condo rescued me from that awful vulture in Egypt. Remember?" *(See Book Five – The Curse of the Mummy's Case.)*

The Bearoness put on her sternest look. "If I hear from Mlle Woof that either of you are trying crazy jumps or leaps, you'll be in big time trouble. Leave that to Otto. He has special talents that you don't have or ever will."

This brought on a fit of ursine pouts until one of the stunt bears fell off the drawbridge into the moat. Eyes went wide, breaths were held, mouths gaped and then the "victim" jumped back up and bowed to the applause of the onlookers. "Wow, he's great. Will he get the job, Momma?"

"That's up to Preston Polar and Herr Schäferhund. They make the decisions. Let's go to the ballroom. We can watch the sword fights."

McTavish lunged at Arabella and then ran up the drawbridge heading for the ballroom. Bella scampered after him followed by the indefatigable Mlle Woof.

Bearyl looked at Belinda and said, "Remember when Bearnice and I thought flying an SST was the best job in the world. Sometimes I wish I was back in the cockpit with the two of you. Now she's singing her heart out; I'm going from dramatic gig to gig and you have a couple of white tigers as your flight crew. Although, I understand they're going to be part of the Feline Felons. That's such a hoot. Chita's been practicing her floozy routine in the bar each night."

The Bearoness replied, "Chita's an original. I think Octavius has finally reconciled himself to the fact that she's a good 'un. I, however, am turning into a fusty old inn keeper."

"Are you kidding, Bel? You and the Aquabears are at your zenith and you have a cushy role in this cinematic extravaganza. Don't give me that 'old inn keeper' stuff. But let's get serious for a moment. I'm wondering whether I'm on the detectives' suspects list as far as Brittany's death is concerned. I guess they might believe I could have pushed her over the balcony in order to get her job. It's no secret I wasn't crazy about her even though I hardly knew her."

Belinda sighed, "I'm afraid you are but you're way at the end of the pack. Where were you this morning when she took her dive?"

"Having breakfast with the scriptwriters. At the time, I was written in for the part of studio head – the one you're going to take. We were trying to get agreement on what her character should be like. We were settling on her having a 'lost cause' crush on Preston or I should say, Barton Bear. Little did we know. If you want to play the part that way, I have copious notes from our discussions."

"So you clearly have an alibi for the time of her death?"

"God, I hope so. I still remember that Canadian fiasco when Bearnice and I were both suspected as murderers. Once around that track is more than enough, thank you." *(See Book Four – The Lower Case)*

"I'll pass that information on to Octavius although I guess they'll still want to hear directly from you and the Racoon Brothers."

"Fine. They are the sweetest guys, by the way. A little crazy but we're used to that, aren't we? I think they'll be wanting to meet up with you shortly."

They had reached the ballroom where McTavish and Arabella were being constrained by the Bichon. "Mes petits, you are not to get in the way. They are performing 'exploits dangereuse' and you and they could get hurt. Votre maman will kill us all if anything happens."

This was not going over with the hyperactive duo until Belinda came on the scene with Bearyl. From the other side of the ballroom, Octavius and I emerged. The Great Bear stared at the Cubs and said two words, "Behave yourselves!"

Bearyl looked at us and said, "I understand you would like to know my whereabouts when Brittany took her fall. As I told Belinda, I was having a working breakfast with the scriptwriters. You can talk to them and get a confirmation."

The Bearoness joined in. "I have to see them about taking on Bearyl's role now that she's replacing Brittany. Come along and we'll talk to them together."

She turned to the Cubs and said, "You heard what your father said. If I hear you have interrupted or gotten in the way, I'll have Dougal lock you up in one of the castle's dungeons."

Arabella laughed. "There aren't any dungeons."

I looked at her. "Wanna bet?"

"Oh, Uncle Maury!!

Chapter Fifteen

Another forensic review
Comes up with few facts that are new.
She was drunk, that we know
When she fell far below.
Are the prints on the rug a good clue?

We found the dramatists hard at work in one of the conference rooms. Bearyl introduced us. "Sheldon and Seymour Racoon, I think you have met these animals but just in case, let me re-introduce Bearoness Belinda Béarnaise Bruin Bear (nee Black) the principal owner of this resort, leader of the Aquabears and your new thespian, replacing me in the role of Bearnadette, the studio chief. I've shared our notes from this morning's session with her. You probably know of this imposing ursine, Doctor Octavius Bear, mate to the Bearoness, gazillionaire owner of Universal Ursine Industries, joint proprietor of Polar Paradise and highly successful detective and crimefighter. I think you've already met Maury Meerkat, Octavius' aide-de-camp who is also our talent agent and a very competent detective."

"Folks, the Racoon Brothers have won many awards for their screen plays and several television series. Preston and Herr Hund are lucky to have them."

Pawshakes all around. Bearyl looked at the Racoons. "It's in their capacity as detectives that they wanted to speak with you."

Octavius rumbled, "Gentlebeasts, sorry to interrupt. Maury and I are helping Superintendent Wardlaw of Shetland Yard and Mr. Fetlock Holmes, the famous horse detective to investigate the unfortunate death of Ms. Brittany. We just wanted to check one thing with you, and we'll let you get back to your creative work. We understand that at the time Ms. Brittany fell from her sixth-floor suite, you two and Bearyl here were having a working breakfast going over her original part as Bearnadette."

Sheldon nodded. "We were at it from seven o'clock until ten. When we heard Brittany was dead and that Bearyl was going to take her part as Bearbara, we agreed to reset and meet again with a different script. We're working on that now. You'll be next on our list, Bearoness, if that's OK with you."

Belinda smiled, "Ready whenever you are."

Seymour commented. "Frankly, it's a pleasure to have an experienced and talented actress like Bearyl in that part. Brittany was badly cast in that role and she wasn't the easiest bear to get along with. She kept insisting on more scenes, lines and close-ups or she'd complain to Preston. She was beautiful but... I shouldn't talk ill of the dead, but I'm not sorry she's gone from the film. Was it an accident? I can't imagine her committing suicide."

I replied, "We believe she was killed, but we don't know by whom!"

*****

As the afternoon wore on, the advocates of law and order met to compare notes. Fetlock Holmes had re-examined the room but found little new. Two additional sets of paw prints in the thick carpet – one ursine and one of nondescript shape – turned out to be from Phoebe Fairbearn and Angela's visit. The crystal drinks bowl on the floor had also been explained by Angela. That left Brittany's prints and those of her unknown assailant. The bed was unmade and showed signs of the actress sprawled on top of the covers. She had probably fallen back after the departure of the two housekeepers. An empty vodka bottle stood on an end table. The balcony doors were slid open, but one panel was off its tracks. An ursine paw print was visible on the glass. Brittany's or her killer's? The balcony guard rail was partially bent, suggesting a pretty powerful force had been used to toss the polar ingenue to her death. The suite was to remain sealed.

Superintendent Wardlaw and the Medical Examiner had gone over the body before sending it down to the Abeardeen Morgue. There was no water in her lungs indicating that she had not drowned. The fall had killed her. The castle is built atop a cliff so her total fall into the ocean from the sixth floor was actually close to 150 feet. Her face, ribs and legs had sustained severe damage. She had obviously imbibed a significant amount of alcohol. There were cuts on her left paw probably caused by grabbing for the sliding door or the railing. Any other bruising brought on during a struggle was difficult to distinguish from her overall wounds. The nails of her front paws were free of any skin or hair that might have come from her opponent. So, we need not look for any one sporting a recent wound or scar.

Octavius and I compared the results of our interviews with Bearyl, Angela, Ms. Fairbearn and the Racoon Brothers. We had dropped them from our list of possibles. The Giant Panda cinematographer, Jane Huang Hau was up on the roof managing the drone when Brittany fell. Doris and Ella, on the other hand, were still active suspects. We all agreed that our next target would have to be Preston Pavel Polar.

Ursula rang her chime to get our attention. "Gentlebeasts. Right now, Preston Polar is with Herr Schäferhund participating in the stunt double auditions. Doris, Ella and Jane Huang Hau are with them along with a crew of production animals. The boars are doing quite well but the females are a bit too small to simulate Ms. Bearyl who is a much larger sow than Ms. Brittany. She was very easy for Preston to lift. I doubt if Ms. Bearyl can slim down to that weight. They may have to resort to costumes and padding on the doubles."

"By the way, I noticed that you have eliminated Herr Schäferhund from your consideration. He is no doubt much smaller and lighter in weight than Ms. Brittany but is still a very powerful animal. he could have attacked and forced her to fall back, especially if she was still hung over."

Fetlock Holmes intervened, "There were no canine prints on the rug, Ms. Ursula. but that is not totally conclusive. Thank you. We shall speak further to Herr Hund."

Chapter Sixteen

The arrival of Bruce Wallaroo
Adds a really great mind to our crew.
He's a highly skilled cop
But his jumping won't stop
And he plays on a didgeridoo.

The stunt tryouts were just wrapping up out in the courtyard. The interior workouts had ended earlier. Two teams were selected. Four crazy polar bears who chose to make their livings flirting with serious injury or even death. I guess it takes all kinds.

When Octavius and I walked up, Preston and Herr Hund were engaged in deep and serious conversation in German. From what I could pick up, Bearyl seemed to be the topic under consideration. German is not my strong suit. On our arrival, the dialogue stopped and they both turned to us.

I asked, "Do you have the stunt doubles all sorted out?"

Preston replied, "Yes, now all we have to do is sort the stunts out. I design them. Gustav here gets them integrated into the scenarios, The Racoon Brothers do their thing with the scripts and Doris and Ella prepare and set up the events."

"Truly major production numbers!"

"But so essential to the success of the film or I should say films, thanks to your brilliant idea."

Octavius grunted. "Gentlebeasts. I am sorry to interrupt your efforts, but we have a killing on our paws and Superintendent Wardlaw, Fetlock Holmes, Maury and I are engaged in finding Ms. Brittany's murderer."

Preston lifted his substantial eyebrow. *(No doubt artificially enhanced. Polar brows are actually rather sparse.)* "You're convinced she was thrown off the balcony?"

"Quite certain, Preston. Either that or she was forced to fall over by her attacker. We are going through the process of eliminating potential suspects and we would like to talk to both of you separately."

"You consider me a suspect? That's nonsense."

"I hope it is. Help us prove it."

"Oh, all right! Gustav, why don't you get started on your list of tasks and I'll speak with these folks. I didn't realize you do double duty as a detective, Doctor Bear. And you too, Maury."

"We've been at it for quite a while."

"Now that I think about it, I can understand why you might think I killed Brittany. She was becoming increasingly difficult to deal with and was threatening to jeopardize the film. We had adjoining rooms on the top floor. I stopped in last night and told her that if she didn't shape up, I was going to fire her. She didn't take it kindly. She had been drinking and accused me of sexual harassment. If anyone was harassing anyone, it was her."

"Preston, at this stage in the film's development would you really have fired her?"

"I certainly didn't want to. Look at all the hassles we are dealing with now that she's gone. But I couldn't use her in her current state. I tried to scare her out of her bitchiness. I thought she was a professional, but I was clearly wrong. If I was going to throw her off the balcony, I would have done it last night. This morning, when you called me, Maury, I was going over the stunt double tryout plans with Doris and Ella."

"They can vouch for you and you for them?"

"Yes, your call and the security officer interrupted us. Obviously, I had to go down to the shore immediately, but I told the PA's to finish up and I'd check back with them later."

Octavius frowned, "Obviously, we'll have to check this out with the two grizzlies,"

"Go to it." He stalked off.

I turned to the Great Bear. "We seem to be up to our ears in interlocking alibis. Is it my suspicious nature or do you also smell a conspiracy?"

Octavius pawsed for a moment, looked at the ceiling and then said, "The thought had crossed my mind. I believe Phoebe, Angela and Bearyl's stories and I think Holmes and Wardlaw would agree. But these others? Who knows? After all, this is a group of actors or would-be actors. Brittany certainly piled up a lot of hostility.

We haven't spoken with Herr Hund yet but before we do, I think a bit of brainstorming might be appropriate. Let's get together with Bel, the Wolves, Chita, Otto and Condo and review the bidding with the Super and the Horse Detective. See if you can arrange a dinner meeting in one of the conference rooms. I'll gather the clan. Don't mention this to any of the film folk, and that includes Bearyl."

I got on the horn with Dougal and the two of us headed down to the kitchens to see if the resident culinary miracle worker, Mrs. McRadish, could pull an impromptu dinner out of her toque.

As I was crossing the entrance to the Great Hall, I heard a familiar voice. "G'day Maury, my bonzer mate. Dougal, gud to seeya! Can I get a room in this gorjus palace?"

It belonged to none other than Chief Inspector Bruce Wallaroo, an irrepressible but brilliant marsupial; an international law and order genius from Down Under and a long-standing associate of mine and the Great Bear's.

"Bruce, welcome! What the hell are you doing here?"

(I will translate the Wallaroo's accent and linguistic gyrations for those of you whose command of Strine is a bit rusty or out and out corroded. It is part of the Narrator's service. No thanks required.)

"I just spent a frustratin' week in Lyon with those bleedin' Interpol bureaucrats tryin' to get an international task force organized to take on a spreadin' rash of crooked social media bozoes. Worldwide scammers. I finally got a move organized but it took all my energy and then some. Figured while I was above the Equator, I'd take a flyer up to Scotland for some R&R and visit the Bearoness and the Cubs. Didn't realize you and the Bear were here, too. Ocko is here, isn't he?"

"Yes, he is. Along with our usual crew. Superintendent Wardlaw and Fetlock Holmes are aboard as well."

"Oh ho! That can only mean one thing. Crime strikes Polar Paradise. What's it this time?"

"A killing. A polar bear movie actress. Remember Preston Pavel Polar from the Christmas Crank Case? He and his crew are here making a film. His ingenue took a dive from a top floor balcony. We're pretty sure it's murder. Come along with Dougal and me. We're going to the kitchen to arrange a working dinner to discuss the situation. I'll bring you up to speed as we go."

"Ta, Mate but I want to get a room and visit the loo first. Where can I meetcha?"

Dougal barked, "The Lauren Bearcall Room in half an hour, Inspector. Drinks, then food."

I turned to the sheepdog. "You're pretty confident that Mrs. McRadish can pull dinner off on such short notice."

"Certainly, Mr. Maury. She's a genius!"

*****

She is and she did. As our team plus law enforcement straggled into the room, Fiona and two dining room waiters rolled in drinks tables from the lounge. The waiters then moved over several side tables for buffet style eating. We arranged the chairs as we wished. Octavius, by dint of his robust voice, got everyone's attention. "I've called this session to make sure we are all on the same page as far as Brittany's death is concerned. We need opinions and different viewpoints. Have a drink. Food will be here shortly, and then we can brainstorm and make suggestions."

At this point the conference room door slammed open and a bounding whirlwind vaulted into the room. "G'day all. Lovely to see you again. Hello, Ocko. I'll have a schooner of beer, Fiona! Where are the Cubs?"

I hadn't mentioned Bruce to Octavius and the Great Bear's look of surprise was worth the price of admission. Belinda laughed. Chita jumped up and hugged the Wallaroo. Frau Schuylkill choked on her bowl of wine. She and the Inspector had issues, at least when he was at the Bear's Lair. The Bear extended a paw and said, "Welcome Inspector. Delighted you're here even though I don't know why." He gave me a puzzled look and I shrugged.

I took up my bowl of fermented coconut milk VSOP and led the Mad Marsupial off to a corner where I proceeded to play out chapter and verse of what had taken place so far and caused our little get together this evening. As he bounced around, I managed to get the story across to him just in time for our menu items to appear.

We all settled in to devour Mrs. McRadish's culinary sorcery. Even the Frau, a Cordon Bleu chef in her own right, was impressed at the quality, diversity and downright deliciousness of the food. The

Bearoness had a real dining room winner in her principal chef. The sheep poked her head into the room to check on us and was greeted with loud applause. A blush and a curtsey and off she went to supervise the kitchens.

"All right," said Octavius, "I think we are all skilled enough to eat, drink, think and talk at the same time. Are we all agreed that we are facing a case of murder here? Her plunge over the rail and into the ocean was certainly not suicide and given the evidence, highly unlikely as an accident."

Nodding heads. Fetlock Holmes whickered and said, "From what we have observed, it looks very much like only one ursine individual was there with her when she fell. I believe she was pushed, not thrown. The bent railing and offset sliding door suggest she was moving at some speed. She may also have been unsteady from a night of drinking and unable to resist."

Chita interposed, "Wouldn't that lend some credence to it being a drunken accident?"

The Horse responded, "I think not. She was propelled. The evidence we got from the maid and chief housekeeper suggest she was still staggering from her imbibing. The guard rail probably would have prevented her from going over if she wasn't pushed."

The Frau asked, "You say 'one ursine individual' based on the prints on the rug. Does that eliminate Herr Schäferhund in your mind?"

"Yes and no," said Octavius, "and this is where some creative thinking is required. Could this be a conspiracy? Brittany was just about universally disliked, perhaps even hated, by the entire cast, crew and management. Preston said he was on the verge of firing her. Herr Hund rejoiced at Bearyl replacing her. The PA's despised her and the scriptwriters found her extremely difficult. They all have alibis but they are vouching for each other."

The Colonel asked, "So you think this was planned? If so, the timing seems strange. Why not kill her off at night? Under cover of darkness. Eight in the morning would not be my favorite time for tossing someone overboard. I think this was a spontaneous act. She was obviously in a foul mood according to Phoebe and Angela. She may have attacked whomever was in the room and they fought back a bit too hard. It may even have been self-defense."

Ursula, who had been party to all this discussion, rang her chime to get attention. "Gentlebeasts, there is the question of the missing laptop. Angela and Phoebe say it was there when they were thrown out of Brittany's room. Where is it now and why is it missing?"

"Good point, Ursie," I said. "Her smart phone was still in the room, wasn't it?"

The Border Collie responded. "Yes, our constable found it. Her last call was early last night to Preston. It lasted less than a minute. There were other calls earlier – to the scriptwriters; the cinematographer; Doris, the PA. She was supposed to be at the stunt double tryouts in the morning. She also used the inside phone system to order up a bottle of vodka."

Otto chirped, "She may have called Preston after he threatened to fire her. She may have been trying to sweet talk her way back into his good graces. I suspect he hung up on her."

Octavius boomed, "We need to find that laptop."

Condo said, "You still have to interview Herr Hund? What about Jane Huang Hau, the Panda cinematographer?"

"She was on the roof with her crew, flying a photographic drone but for the sake of completeness, we should interview her as well. The drone briefly picked up Brittany's body falling into the ocean."

Bruce, who was jumping around as usual - only this time balancing his third schooner of beer - burbled, "Sounds to me like you ought to get the whole crew together and see if their stories still check out. Somebody may contradict somebody or engage in a little blame-throwing."

Holmes agreed. "It sounds like our next best step."

Belinda, who had been listening up to this point, wondered, "Do you think she may have been blackmailing someone? How did she get the job in the first place if she was such a hateful no-talent? There are scads of beautiful polar sows just dying to take on a role in a Preston Polar extravaganza. Ursula, can you do some deeper background checks on the players, please. I'm going to go check on the Cubs. Goodness knows what they may be up to. Then I have a date with the scriptwriters. Bearnadette is coming to life."

As she left the room, the assemblage broke up into smaller groups. Octavius, Chita, Condo and I sat down with Bruce and got caught up on his latest escapades. He confided that he had ditched his harmonica and was taking lessons on playing the didgeridoo. Oh joy! The Wolves were talking with Holmes and Wardlaw. Otto was chatting with Ursula and the last round of drinks was being consumed. Down in the courtyard the set designers and crew were breaking down the structures used for the stunt tryouts. The Feline Felons, minus Chita, were doing their thing to the delight of the Lounge patrons…and a murderer was still on the loose.

Chapter Seventeen

The Octavians all are go-go
Getting ready to start the big show.
But I can't explain this.
The sow's laptop's amiss.
Did it fall in the sea far below?

Dawn spread its rosy fingers over the sea, windswept cliffs, forests, braes and Polar Paradise castle. Since I was in bed with a pillow over my head, I saw none of it. Down in the extended courtyard, a helicopter was running up its engines preparing to take Fetlock Holmes and Superintendent Wardlaw back to Abeardeen and then, in Holmes' case, back to London. The Super would return shortly. Other demands and pressures had imposed themselves and with Octavius, Chief Inspector Wallaroo, the local constabulary and the rest of our investigative team still here, they felt confident in leaving the Brittany mystery in our capable paws for the nonce.

But we were at a standstill although the Great Bear had taken Bruce's suggestion and arranged for a joint sit down with the production team later in the week. To my knowledge, no one else had departed the hotel by way of a balcony or window and there was a creeping sensation among the inhabitants that whoever had tossed the young polar sow had done the production company and perhaps the world a big favor. Not much maudlin hypocrisy here.

Nevertheless, a crime of the worst kind had been committed and the Octavians are dedicated to bringing wrongdoers to justice. The Wolves, Bruce, Ursula and I were devoting much of our attention on the problem. It just didn't look like there would be a speedy resolution.

Meanwhile, work on the films within films was accelerating. Additional crew, equipment and structures were building up. Ella had imported a costume department from Preston's studio near Moscow.

Ballrooms, conference centers and outdoor sites were being commandeered. The Aquabears and Otto were rehearsing for their performances in the indoor pools. Bedrooms were filling up with casts, crew, hangers-on and cinema-struck tourists. The kitchens and bars were operating at full tilt and the locals from Unst and Baltasound were being marshalled for their duties as extras. Drones and choppers were being set up to shoot outdoor sequences and Jane Huang Hau had tripled her staff to make up first and second filming units.

Herr Hund had fallen in love with Lion, Unicorn and their pub and had insisted that a sequence with Preston and those two worthies be shot on the premises. Not sure how Preston felt about being upstaged by a Unicorn, but it made for great publicity. "Unicorns do exist. See him and his Lion sidekick mixing it up with Preston Pavel Polar." The press releases were already out, and a television crew had flown in from Moscow to cover the event.

In the meantime, Bearyl, Belinda, Chita, Lepi, Jake, Ben, Gal, Otto and Condo were all taken up with rehearsals, script changes, costumes and makeup. Octavius finally came around and agreed to play the rival studio heavy who employed the Five Feline Felons. He was a riot dressed in an oversized plaid suit and chomping on a cigar. I have photos available for a modest fee.

Personal opinion! I think Preston may have been losing control of the situation and too many places, situations and personalities bode likely to upstage the matinee idol. Oh well, there is always the cutting room floor. Needless to say, most of the participants were having a ball.

And then there were the Cubs. They had managed to ensnare the PA's, Herr Hund, the Racoon Brothers and the camera crews with their nth degree cuteness. Suddenly, Bearnadette, the studio chief played by Belinda had two children written into the script. Her husband had died and left her a single mother who had a severe crush on Barton

Bear, played by Preston. Mlle Woof also had a part as the Cubs' governess.

Dougal, Phoebe Fairbearn, Mrs. McRadish, Fiona, Harold and the entire hotel staff, bless their collective hearts, dealt with the chaos like the real champs that they were. However, I believe this is going to be the first and last motion picture shot at Polar Paradise. But who knows?

Let me not suggest that while all this folderol was going on, no time was being spent trying to unravel Brittany's death. Belinda's blackmail theory was being pursued by Ursula and as you might expect among movie folks, a number of juicy and/or unsavory stories were unfolding.

Most of the stories clustered around Preston. It seems his sex symbol image was backed up by a series of adventures and misadventures, mates and mistresses, angry husbands, payments to kill stories and lawsuits. He also seemed to run through agents with great alacrity. While currently unattached, he had been married three times. It's not clear what his true relationship with Brittany was. No doubt, she imagined it to be "the real thing." I suspect he thought differently.

Herr Schäferhund, by contrast, was a sexual straight arrow. Mated for years to one female. Not known to play around but he had one serious vice – he gambled. Currently, he was in debt for some rather amazing sums to some not-so-amazing people. It was pretty common knowledge.

The writers were into drugs, but they seemed to be keeping it under control. No overdoses or bizarre events. Doris had one scrape with the law for shoplifting. The studio bought her out of it. Ella has a clean slate.

Jane Huang Hau was known to drink a bit to excess but her big issue was overeating. No bamboo forest was safe with her around. She had an arrangement with the hotel kitchen staff to have a very large supply of bamboo shoots at the ready at all times. For this she paid extravagantly. Unfortunately, her intake of bamboo forces her, like all of her species, to head for the bathroom with great frequency. Strange creatures, these Pandas!

In the course of her search, Ursula discovered that the Giant Panda was up for the Cinematographer of the Year Award given by the International Film Council. She had won it twice in the past. Most of her work consists of deep mood pieces. This current rumbustious effort is not her normal mode. But, as I said, a Panda has to eat, especially this ravenous Panda. It's her first outing with Preston but so far, so good.

Herr Hund was also an award winner. He produced a series of historical studies that traced the early migrations of different species after the Big Shock. They are still regarded as definitive after a long period in circulation.

Preston, on the other hand, didn't win awards. He just made a lot of money.

Which brings us to Brittany. Professionally, she started out as a model. She had a number of on-and-off romances as you might expect and was briefly married to a Polar bit part player who got her into the film business. They divorced in short order. Her walk-on appearances as an ingenue were highly forgettable and it's not quite clear why Preston chose her for this part. One can only speculate. Our lawyer, Wolford, had asked Sasha Sable about Brittany's contract and was told that she was working on a contingency basis for this one film. That seemed to be Preston's style. So Brittany was by no means guaranteed a long and profitable movie career. She might have ended up slinging hash after this epic was in the can.

The young sow seemed to have real talent for making enemies. Just about everyone on the film team and most of the hotel staff who had to deal with her couldn't stand her.

If anything, Ursula's inquiries were producing fruit–in fact, a whole damn orchard. But they weren't helping us cut down our suspects list. Complications, complications.

Octavius had emerged from the costume department and was eager to shed his film tycoon suit and cigar before the Cubs caught sight of him. Belinda didn't help any by falling into paroxysms of uncontrollable laughter when she saw him. I was afraid he was going to back off on his promise to perform but I think his own sense of humor *(he has one)* kicked in. He didn't seem to mind playing Poppa Bear in the recent Goldilocks Christmas Pantomime, but he may have done that for the Cubs.

I had Ursula give him her Suspects Report.

"Well, that's all very interesting but it's not getting us any closer to a conclusion. I still want to know what happened to Brittany's laptop. Did it end up in the ocean?"

I had asked Harold to take two of the constables out for a shallow dive near where the body had been floating but the computer could have dropped anywhere in the area. Anyway, no joy! I think the killer has it or may have destroyed it. I believe it's time for a little surreptitious room searching. I'll have to get Bruce going on that one. He represents law enforcement. I'm just a nosy amateur detective. *(but a pretty good one!)*

The Great Bear looked bemused. "Is Brittany's room still sealed?"

"I think so."

"I want to go back and take another look at those paw prints on the rug. Holmes and Wardlaw examined them the last time. Neither of them is an ursine and I think they may have missed some subtle differences in the sets of prints. Get Phoebe Fairbearn to come with us."

I got on the house phone and asked The Chief Housekeeper to meet us at the sixth-floor suite where the Polar ingenue took her dive. Octavius and I went off in search of the freight elevator *(goods lift)* that would accommodate his weight and size. Phoebe was waiting for us with a card key when we finally arrived.

"Is there something I can do for you, Doctor Bear?"

"Yes, Ms. Fairbearn, I want to examine your feet – actually your pawprints. On the rug in this suite."

"Do you suspect me of something?"

He chuckled, "No, not at all. I want to do a comparison. Your paws are not quite the same size as Brittany's. I think they're a bit bigger. I want to eliminate the pawprints you made when you were in here with Angela and make sure we are looking at the victim's prints. Could you just walk over there by the bathroom door? Thank you."

I looked at Phoebe's prints and the ursine impressions at the sliding door to the balcony. They were different. "OK," I said, "let's sort these out. It looks like Brittany went backwards from the side of the bed, out and over the balcony rail. There's another set of forward-facing prints that cross over hers." I scratched my nose. They were ursine prints, but a couple were different. Same five claws but it looked like they also had a sixth thumb-like protrusion. Strange!

Octavius did another one of his signature "Hmmms."

"Know any six clawed bears, Maury?"

"Nope, only two and three toed sloths."

Phoebe looked confused. "Is there anything else I can do to help, gentlebeasts?"

"I don't think so, Phoebe. Don't be concerned. You and Angela are in the clear. Did she come into work today?"

"Oh aye, Doctor Bear. She's very conscientious."

"And so are you. Thank you again."

"Maury, let's go find that laptop."

Chapter Eighteen

Let us ask a grave question right now
Of the Multiverse Project and how
New electrons appear.
For it isn't quite clear
What the physical laws will allow.

Time Out! We are overdue to touch base with our Multiverse mavens in Cincinnati. Ursula is managing a conference call between The Bear's Lair and Polar Paradise. Howard, the Porcupine genius and his equally brainy Dolphin sidekick, Marlin, are on one end and Octavius, the Colonel and I are on the other. The Multiverse Project which is exploring quantum entangling activities of electrons between alternate universes has been a partial success but also a source of serious issues.

We believed our original target world, Biosphere X, was uninhabited. We were wrong. It's for the birds. It has a population of paranoid and dangerously aggressive avian leaders who saw our work as an intolerable invasion of their "Homeworld." Otto was instrumental in uncovering their nature and intentions.

After a set of near fatal encounters with the murderous denizens of Biosphere X, we managed to subdue them. Ursula killed off two winged assassins as they tried to firebomb the Bear's mansion and the surrounding estate. *(See Book Seven - The Suit Case.)* This was followed by a devastating attack on the leadership of Biosphere X by General Turmoil in retaliation for their attacks on his group.

General Turmoil is a Horse. *(We call him Crazy Horse.)* He leads a clandestine, ostensibly non-existent, semi-governmental agency known as the Business. He and his group have a very high level of interest in the Multiverse and the resources to go with it. Although

117

he denies it, his apparent motivation seems to be conquering the cosmos.

At one point, while still in the Army, Colonel Wyatt Where was compelled to participate in a series of other-world transit experiments designed by the scientists in the Business. They eventually deemed the experiments a failure and shut them down. However, unknown to the General, Wyatt did succeed in traveling to alternative universes. He escaped from the Business and after several intervening occupations, ended up with Octavius. He makes periodic visits to other worlds as part of The Bear's Multiverse Project in cooperation with Howard Watt and Marlin the Dolphin.

Now, Marlin and Howard have selected another supposedly uninhabited Multiverse venue we are calling Biosphere Z. They have installed a quantum generator on the planet and are conducting transit experiments. However, they have discovered that electrons teleporting from Biosphere Z are appearing in regular sequences and what seems to be purposeful intervals. Suggestion: There may be an intelligence there managing the process. Who??

Octavius believes it is one of General Turmoil's agents. The Colonel and I agree.

General Turmoil and Octavius have crossed paths and swords many times. Mutual detestation but also grudging mutual respect. The General is constantly trying to acquire our information and processes, more often than not, dishonestly. This activity from Biosphere Z might be another example.

Fortunately, we don't believe he knows about Ursula. He would spend an immense amount of time, money and effort to acquire the AGI system. Meanwhile, we need to find out who or what is sending those Biosphere Z electrons.

The Bear rumbled. "Howard? Maury, the Colonel and I all agree with your suspicion that the electron stream from Biosphere Z may be happening courtesy of General Turmoil. Is there any way we can positively determine that's the case?"

The Porcupine responded. "We're going to send a stream back out there and see what kind of response we get. If we get a cogent, non-random, meaningful reaction, it means someone intelligent and knowledgeable is at the wheel and this is not an accident."

"Well," said Octavius, "that will prove we were wrong about Biosphere Z being uninhabited, but it still doesn't prove it's the General. On the other hand, there aren't too many animals well-informed and capable enough to participate in these experiments. At least that we know about. Are you investigating any other worlds?'

"We have two other targets that look promising. Marlin is working up plans and resources for establishing contact. We'll let you know via Ursula if and when we get through."

"OK, give it a shot and let's discuss it further. We're about to get tangled up in some movie-making here at the castle. Who knows? There may be parts for a Porcupine and a Dolphin. Take care. Regards to Marlin."

The Development of Civilization

Volume Ten - Part Three

Adventures Among the Electrons

(From "An Introduction to Faunapology" by
Octavius Bear Ph.D.)

Most animals have a rudimentary familiarity with Physics, the natural science that seeks to find and precisely define relationships among the most fundamental measurable quantities in the universe. It involves the study of matter and its motion and behavior through space and time, along with related concepts such as energy and force. We are pretty comfortable with those phenomena that we can see, hear, taste, touch or mentally visualize. We have an incomplete but usually sufficient understanding of electricity, magnetism, hydraulics, optics and sound, for example, to lead our lives without too much concern. It's when the dimensions of the universe expand incredibly (intergalactic space, black holes, light speed) or contract to the infinitesimal that we get nervous and often want to hide somewhere.

The atom was once thought to be the absolutely indivisible makeup of the universe. Turns out it's not. There's a lot going on inside the atom. That's what Particle Physics is all about. Often referred to as Quantum Physics, scientists have been exploring, quantifying and cataloguing sub-atomic components with exotic names like fermions, quarks and leptons. One form of lepton, the electron, may sound familiar because it has been used and misused in all sorts of situations.

Near the end of the twentieth century, to put a little order into this apparent chaos, scientists pulled everything they knew about

Quantum Physics into one massive equation — the **Standard Model of Particle Physics**. *It is very much a work in progress. So far, twelve basic particles have been identified but they can be combined into more complex entities. In addition to the particles, there are also four fundamental forces that propel this part of the universe: the strong force, weak force, the electromagnetic force, and gravity. Unfortunately, gravity is not a good fit for the Standard Model. The other three forces are supported by particles known as bosons. A major use of the Standard Model is not just to identify and catalog. It has a major predictive role.*

In 2012, the so-called Higgs boson that provides particles with mass and had been predicted by the Model was found at CERN's Large Hadron Collider. CERN is the European Organization for Nuclear Research. The Large Hadron Collider (LHC) is the world's largest and most powerful particle accelerator to date. It is made up of a 27-kilometre ring of superconducting magnets with a number of accelerating structures to boost the energy of the particles along the way. The LHC primarily collides proton beams. Inside the accelerator, two high-energy particle beams travel at close to the speed of light before they are made to collide. The beams travel in opposite directions in separate beam pipes – two tubes kept at **ultrahigh vacuum.** *The result of the collision may be a new particle or boson.*

Currently, groundwork is starting up for another collider further in the future, known as the High-Luminosity LHC. That upgrade, expected to be ready by 2026, will increase the rate of collisions by at least a factor of five.

There is a massive amount of literature, some of it understandable by the average bear, dealing with Particle Physics. I recommend you do some browsing, if you are so inclined!

You well may ask: "Does Particle Physics have any practical application beyond keeping a lot of scientists and engineers very busy and spending a lot of money on exotic equipment?" The answer is "Yes!"

Consider biomedicine and drug development; cancer therapy; diagnostic instruments; nuclear monitoring; turbulence analysis and prediction; nuclear batteries; enhanced power transmission; computing and telecommunications tools; cryptographic and other security technologies; super enhanced light sources, just to name a few.

"Though she be but little, she is fierce." William Shakesbeare: Midsummer Night's Dream

Chapter Nineteen

Fetlock Holmes thinks that Brittany's fall
Had been caused by a push and that's all.
If that theory proves true
We have more work to do
And more suspects that we have to call.

Back to our search for Brittany's computer. Bruce Wallaroo called Superintendent Wardlaw in Abeardeen. He in turn got a search warrant to look through all the film crew's rooms and transmitted it to us at the castle. The Super was coming back to Polar Paradise later today. I placed a call to Fetlock Holmes in London and shared our thoughts based on the pawprints in Brittany's room. He agreed that she was probably pushed or otherwise propelled backwards rather than lifted by animal or animals unknown. He made the point that the assailant need not have been larger or heavier than Brittany. He, she (or they?) only needed speed and leverage to get her off balance. Once she was flailing, a solid push would have sufficed.

That observation left us with a different set of priorities. Her killer didn't necessarily have to be bigger or stronger. We needed to talk with Herr Schäferhund although it didn't seem his pawprints were on the rug. We decided to split our resources. Bruce and Sergeant Alistair who had stayed behind when the Police returned to Abeardeen would conduct the room searches. They, after all, represented law enforcement and had the power of the search warrant on their side. Octavius, the Wolves and I would talk with Herr Hund.

The canine producer was not happy to be taken away from his overflowing list of activities. The film was nearing that inevitable point of flying off the rails into chaos unless he and the PA's could keep it on track.

"Where was I when Brittany fell from the balcony? Let's see. I had just gone over the plans for the stunt double tryouts and was directing the scenic crew in building the traps, walls and jumping off points for the stunts. I was on my way out to the moat and drawbridge to check on the set-ups there when Preston called me on my smartphone. Brittany had taken her spill."

The Frau, all business, asked, "Can anyone vouch for your presence during that period, Herr Hund?"

"Talk to any of the crew. I was certainly on their case to get the environments set up. We started at seven and were still at it when Preston called. Thank heaven we were ready in time for the tryouts. Preston is insistent on having the stunts perfect. It's his signature. Besides his noble profile, of course. The auditions had to be absolutely authentic."

"So you couldn't have gotten to Brittany's room during that period?"

"I resent the implication. I didn't even have breakfast."

*****

Thus far the room searches had turned up nothing but irate individuals who felt their privacy was being violated *(which it was!)* While the objective of the search was Brittany's laptop, a few other items like drug and liquor stashes had come to light. The Chief Inspector and Sergeant decided to overlook their findings. One other item brought on a laugh. Jane Huang Hau's room was stacked floor to ceiling with photographic equipment, film cases. computers and piles and piles of bamboo. The Panda clearly had an eating compulsion. The computers turned out to be all the property of the film company. Not the one they were searching for.

When we got back together and compared our fruitless results, The Colonel called up Ursula.

"Yes, Colonel Where? What can I do for you?"

"Ursula, can you read back our interview with Jane Huang Hau, please?"

"We don't have one. Colonel. Nobody has spoken with her since we first took up the drone's footage of the scenery and the partial shots of Ursula's fall."

"Nobody has questioned her?"

"Not on the record. I think you all assumed that since she was on the roof with her crew, there was nothing more to discuss."

I cut in. "Ursula, I'm interested in one set of pawprints we found on Brittany's rug. Are there any six-toed ursines that you know about?" This produced some quizzical looks from the Wolves and the Police.

The AGI responded, "Yes and no, Maury. There is one bear that has a projection on their front paws at the wrist. It looks like an extra toe but it's not really."

"Just the front paws? What bear is that?"

"The Panda!"

We all looked at each other. Octavius snorted. "I think we need to talk with Ms. Hau right away."

I interrupted, "Before we do, let's talk with her two Ferret assistants, Freddy and Frank."

"Right. Get a hold of them."

That wasn't as easy as it sounded. All three of them were taken up with making tests of Bearyl. Herr Hund was also there. The Colonel approached Frank who was standing by while Freddy and Jane took shots of the Polar actress.

"Are you Freddy or Frank?"

"I'm Frank. Freddy is the animal with the camera over there with Jane."

"I'm Colonel Wyatt Where," said the Wolf, "and these gentlebeasts are Chief Inspector Bruce Wallaroo of the International Police Force and Maury Meerkat, Doctor Octavius Bear's associate.

"I've met Mr. Meerkat. We made a copy of the drone's footage from that morning and gave him the original. When are we getting that back, by the way?

"I hope shortly. We're investigating the death of Ms. Brittany. This is just routine. We're interviewing everyone on the Preston Polar team to see if they can shed any light on just what happened."

"What did happen? I know she fell off her balcony, but nobody has said whether she jumped, fell or was pushed."

"We're pretty sure she didn't jump or fall accidentally."

"So you're looking for someone who pushed or threw her over? It wasn't me. I was up on the roof controlling our scenery drone. You can ask Freddy."

"What about Jane."

"She wasn't there at that moment. She had gone to her room to use the loo. Those damn bamboo shoots have her running all day long."

"How long was she gone?"

"Ten-fifteen minutes, maybe."

"Thanks, Frank. We'll speak with Freddy and Jane as soon as they finish."

So we waited. I didn't want to interrupt Bearyl's test shots. All of her acting up to this point had been on stage and this was her chance to prove that in addition to her dramatic skills, she was also photogenic. That seemed to be the only thing Brittany had going for her. The camera liked her. Nobody else did.

Finally, they took a break. It appeared the camera liked Bearyl too. I walked over to Freddy and asked him to speak with us. I gave him the "just routine" routine and he confirmed that only he and Frank were on the roof when Brittany took her plunge. Jane had gone to her room, ostensibly to use the facilities. She had returned in time to meet us later when we came calling.

The Colonel, Bruce and I approached the cinematographer and told her we were just closing the loop on all of our inquiries.

Bruce casually remarked on Freddy and Frank claiming she'd been gone from the roof while the drone was taking shots of the castle and picking up Brittany's fall. He asked where she was. It's tough to pick up expressions on a Panda's face. Their eyes are surrounded by a field of black and their mouths seem to be in a perpetual smile.

She pawsed for a moment and said, "I guess I was in my room using the loo. Diarrhea is the Panda's curse. All that bamboo."

The Colonel stared at her and asked, "Are you sure you weren't in Brittany's room?"

"Of course not! What would I be doing there?"

"There were ursine paw prints on the rug in her room."

"Well, sure. She's a bear. Or was!"

"One set of prints were rather peculiar, however. Six claws. I notice that your front paws have a sort of claw on the wrists. I think that's true of all pandas. Would you come with us, please, to Brittany's suite so we can compare your prints?"

"I don't think so. Who are you guys, really? What's your authority?"

I had heard a helicopter landing in the courtyard, and I replied. "We have a search warrant from the Abeardeen Police. Chief Inspector Wallaroo here is from Interpol and we are expecting Superintendent Wardlaw of Shetland Yard-Abeardeen to return to the castle shortly. We can wait for him if you insist on talking to someone with full jurisdiction and authority. Meanwhile, one of us will stay with you to make sure you don't tamper with evidence. You don't happen to know what happened to Brittany's laptop computer, do you?"

"Why would I know that or even care?"

"We believe that laptop had something to do with her death."

Just then, a bearded collie walked into the room. "Hello, All! Ms. Hau, I presume! I'm Superintendent Nigel Wardlaw of Shetland Yard. We have a few questions we need to ask. Would you come with us to Ms. Brittany's suite, please? It's just down the hall."

"I protest, Superintendent. I had nothing to do with that Polar Princess' death."

"Well, we'd like to prove that and remove you from our suspects list. Follow me, please."

As we were making our way out of the cinematographer's suite, Ursula rang the chime on her laptop that I was carrying. I hung back.

"Yes, Ursie?"

"Maury, ask her about Panda Porn!

"Panda Porn?"

"Yes. It's important."

I caught up with the parade just as it was entering the Late Brittany's suite.

"Ms. Hau," the Superintendent began, "There are several peculiar ursine pawprints on the rug in here, coming in the door and facing the balcony. They are mixed in with what we believe are Ms. Brittany's prints facing away from the balcony. Would you walk over here on all fours, please?"

"I have never been in this room, Superintendent. I don't know who those prints belong to."

"And yet they match the prints on the floor in size and configuration. Several have that sixth toe that's peculiar to Pandas. To my knowledge, you're the only Panda here at this hotel."

"All right! I was here that morning. She wanted to persuade me to do more close-ups of her and linger on for longer shots."

"Why did you deny being here at first?"

"I didn't want to be involved."

"Did you agree to her demands?"

"No, Preston would never have signed off."

"You know that for a fact?"

"We've had long discussions on priorities in these films. Personal close-ups are Preston's specialty. The camera has to be in love with him."

"You just had a discussion with her? There was no violence, pushing or shoving?"

A brief hesitation. "No! The whole thing lasted a couple of minutes."

Let me ask again, "Do you know the whereabouts of her laptop computer."

Another brief hesitation. "I don't know anything about it or where it is."

"Probably not! One of my constables found a laptop with her initials etched into it stuffed inside a chair cushion out on the balcony. The hard drive had been wiped clean. There were several sets of pawprints on it, including a set with six claws. The murderer probably hid it there until he or she could recover it without being seen. But we had the rooms sealed. Now. Care to change your story?"

I intervened. "Ms. Hau. What can you tell me about Panda Porn?"

She turned to me. It was tough to tell but I think she was shocked.

"You know about that? How did you find out? Did she tell you?"

"No, I have my own sources. But Brittany knew about your involvement, didn't she?

(Note to Reader: <u>Panda Pornography</u> is real. Look up Google or Wikipedia. Pandas have exceedingly low-level libidos and may only copulate once a year, if then. Attempts are being made to increase the frequency and effectiveness through various experiments, including surgery, egg transfer and showing subjects pictures of males and females performing the sex act – <u>Panda Porn</u>.)

"She knew. She had one of the films I had shot for a fertility lab under a different name when I was younger and needed money. She showed it to me on her laptop. She was going to blackmail me with it. She didn't want money. She wanted me to increase the amount and quality of screen time she had in the two movies."

"But why? The Porn film wasn't illegal, was it?"

"No, but she threatened to send it to the Award Selection Committee of the International Film Council for the Cinematographer of the Year prize. I was favored to win. Three times in a row. Never happened before. That porn film would have killed it."

"So you killed _her_!"

"I didn't mean to. I just wanted to get that laptop out of her paws. I grabbed at it. She swung at me and I pushed her hard. She fell back and after trying to grab the sliding door, she fell over the fence. I stood there shocked, but then I came to my senses. She had dropped the laptop. I grabbed it and formatted the hard drive. Then I stuffed it in the chair cushion until I could safely dispose of it and ran back up to roof just in time to bring in the drone."

The Super shook his head. "I'm afraid you're going to have to come with me, Ms. Hau. We need to look into this further. I'm not sure what charges will be brought against you, but I doubt if you'll be getting the cinematographer award this year."

Pandas do shed tears.

Epilogue

Now you know who our real killer is
It's a highly professional Ms.
What's her fate gonna be?
It's an unknown to me.
Let's return to our work in show-biz.

We stood and watched as the Police helicopter carrying Jane Huang Hau, the Superintendent, Sergeant Alistair and the Constables rose from the helipad and headed southwest to Abeardeen.

I looked at Octavius and asked, "What do you think they'll charge her with?"

"That's up to the Procurator Fiscal *(Scottish equivalent of a US District Attorney.)* The indictments could range from deliberate murder or manslaughter to accidental death or even self-defense. I'm sure they'll be investigating this one for a while."

We turned back to the castle and entered the conference room that was serving as headquarters for the production team.

"This film is cursed." Preston Pavel Polar was roaring. "First our ingenue and now our cinematographer. If we hadn't already invested so much time, money and resources in this thing, I would shut it down."

I sincerely doubt he would, but I didn't say anything. Herr Hund had sprung into action and was flying in Lukas Lynx – a Swedish cinematographer he had worked with several times in the past. He'd be replacing Jane Huang Hau. The camera units were still active and shooting schedules for the next several days had been worked out by Preston, the Schäferhund and the PA's.

Ursula rang her chime and I skittered to the back of the conference room. "What's up, Oh, source of all knowledge?"

"What's your guess on them finishing the film?"

"You're the one with the Probability Algorithms. What do you think?

"I'd say it's likely and with the current cast, it'll may well be a hit."

"By the way, how did you know about the Panda Porn film? I didn't know what the hell I was talking about when I asked Jane that question."

"Deep Data Background Check. She wasn't as careful with that information as she thought."

"It's a shame. She was doing it for science."

"And to keep herself in bamboo. I wonder what they'll do with all those shoots in her room?"

"They'll find another Panda and sell them. Let me change the subject, Ursula. What is going on with Howard and Marlin back at the Bear's Lair? Has anything new happened with Project Multiverse?"

"Funny you should bring that up, Maury. It seems General Turmoil has disappeared."

"As in 'Nobody knows where he is or what happened to him' disappeared?"

"You've got it."

"Any theories?"

"You may remember we believed that the regular procession of electrons coming from Biosphere Z was the work of the Business. We also thought the biosphere was otherwise uninhabited. We may have been wrong on both counts. Our rig is still active, but it was placed there primarily in detect mode. We have been sending electrons from Earth and looking for responses. We started getting unsolicited transmissions initiated by someone or something on the planet. If we are getting them, so is the General. Or so we believe. His folks may be sending them. Knowing his personality, he's not going to let that go unexamined. For that matter neither are we. The difference is Howard and Marlin are still in the Cincinnati Lab, but General Turmoil is missing from his office in Washington. Interplanetary foul play or clandestine activity on the Business' part?"

"How do you know all this?"

"Oh, Maury, come on! Need you ask?"

"Sorry. Ms. Omniscience. So what's happening?"

"The General's second in command, Colonel Jupiter, who is also a horse, has been stirring up the security types. The search is on. Now, either they are engaging in some elaborate play-acting to cover up a calculated plot or someone has captured or done the General in. Remember he staged an attack on the ruling birds on Biosphere X in retaliation for their raids in Boston. They may now be taking their own revenge."

"Is Octavius aware of any of this."

The AGI responded, "I'll brief Octavius on the General after his session with the great matinee idol."

*****

OK, since this is the Epilogue, let's tie up a few loose ends and send this magnum opus off to the publisher.

First, the cinema team has wrapped up filming here and is back at Preston's studios in Moscow doing interior shooting. Some of our newly created stars are there including Bearyl, Belinda, the Cubs,

Condo and the Feline Felons. The new cinematographer, Lukas Lynx, was ecstatic about the opportunity to capture the cats on film. Chita appeared as a panther.

Next, Polar Paradise is settling back down to its calm and hospitable ways. Belinda, Dougal and Phoebe Fairbearn have all agreed that she will be re-employed on a permanent basis. Angela is now the head of domestic staff for the sixth floor. She's still a bit touchy about entering what was once Brittany's room. Dougal has found a buyer for Jane Huang Hau's bamboo supply and is passing on the proceeds for her defense fund. Oh, yes, a large conference of ursine dentists is about to hit the hotel. It seems the fatal and near-fatal events of the past year have actually increased the appeal of the place. Go figure!

Jane Huang Hau's trial has not yet been docketed. The wheels of justice turn slowly.

Octavius, the Wolves and I will be heading back to Cincinnati in a couple of days on the Ursa Major, Octavius' super-sized, C-5A stealth transport. The Bearoness' SST is in Moscow with the thespians.

There are several copies of Ursula with us as well as in Moscow. She is being very mysterious about what she thinks our next adventure will be. Her Predictive Circuits are working overtime.

Finally, we have no new news about General Turmoil. Octavius is not sorry to see him missing but is damned curious about where and how he is. Stay tuned and be on the lookout for Volume Eleven -The Wurst Case Scenario!

The End of

Volume Ten of the

Casebooks of Octavius Bear

The Camera Case

About the Author

Harry DeMaio is a *nom de plume* of Harry B. DeMaio, successful author of several books on Information Security and Business Networks as well as the ten-volume *Casebooks of Octavius Bear for Mx Publishing.* He is also a published author for Belanger Books and the MX Sherlock Holmes series edited by David Marcum. A retired business executive, former consultant, information security specialist, pilot, disk jockey and graduate school adjunct professor, he whiles away his time traveling and writing preposterous books, articles and stories. He has appeared on many radio and TV shows and is an accomplished, frequent public speaker.

Former New York City natives, he and his extremely patient and helpful wife, Virginia, and their Bichon Frisé, Woof, live in Cincinnati (and several other parallel universes.) They have two sons, living in Scottsdale, Arizona and Cortlandt Manor, New York, both of whom are quite successful and quite normal, thus putting the lie to the theory that insanity is hereditary.

His e-mail is hdemaio@zoomtown.com. You can also find him on Facebook. His website is www.octaviusbearslair.com

His books are available on Amazon, Barnes and Noble, directly from MX Publishing and at other fine bookstores.

Also from MX Publishing

The Detective and The Woman Series

  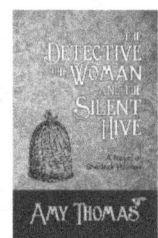 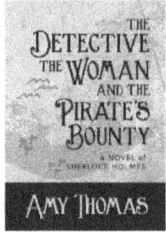

The Detective and The Woman

The Detective, The Woman and The Winking Tree

The Detective, The Woman and The Silent Hive

The Detective, The Woman and The Pirate's Bounty

"The book is entertaining, puzzling and a lot of fun. I believe the author has hit on the only type of long-term relationship possible for Sherlock Holmes and Irene Adler. The details of the narrative only add force to the romantic defects we expect in both of them and their growth and development are truly marvelous to watch. This is not a love story. Instead, it is a coming-of-age tale starring two of our favorite characters."

Philip K Jones

Also from MX Publishing

The Sherlock Holmes and Enoch Hale Series

The Amateur Executioner
The Poisoned Penman
The Egyptian Curse

"The Amateur Executioner: Enoch Hale Meets Sherlock Holmes", the first collaboration between Dan Andriacco and Kieran McMullen, concerns the possibility of a Fenian attack in London. Hale, a native Bostonian, is a reporter for London's Central News Syndicate - where, in 1920, Horace Harker is still a familiar figure, though far from revered. "The Amateur Executioner" takes us into an ambiguous and murky world where right and wrong aren't always distinguishable. I look forward to reading more about Enoch Hale."
Sherlock Holmes Society of London

Also from MX Publishing

When the papal apartments are burgled in 1901, Sherlock Holmes is summoned to Rome by Pope Leo XII. After learning from the pontiff that several priceless cameos that could prove compromising to the church, and perhaps determine the future of the newly unified Italy, have been stolen, Holmes is asked to recover them. In a parallel story, Michelangelo, the toast of Rome in 1501 after the unveiling of his Pieta, is commissioned by Pope Alexander VI, the last of the Borgia pontiffs, with creating the cameos that will bedevil Holmes and the papacy four centuries later. For fans of Conan Doyle's immortal detective, the game is always afoot. However, the great detective has never encountered an adversary quite like the one with whom he crosses swords in "The Vatican Cameos.."

"An extravagantly imagined and beautifully written Holmes story"
(**Lee Child**, NY Times Bestselling author, Jack Reacher series)

Also from MX Publishing

During the elaborate funeral for Queen Victoria, a group of Irish separatists breaks into Westminster Abbey and steals the Coronation Stone, on which every monarch of England has been crowned since the 14th century. After learning of the theft from Mycroft, Sherlock Holmes is tasked with recovering the stone and returning it to England. In pursuit of the many-named stone, which has a rich and colorful history, Holmes and Watson travel to Ireland in disguise as they try to infiltrate the Irish Republican Brotherhood, the group they believe responsible for the theft. The story features a number of historical characters, including a very young Michael Collins, who would go on to play a prominent role in Irish history; John Theodore Tussaud, the grandson of Madame Tussaud; and George Bradley, the dean of Westminster at the time of the theft. There are also references to a number of other Victorian luminaries, including Joseph Lister and Frederick Treves.

Also from MX Publishing

Here is a collection of five previously unknown cases from the astonishing career of the consulting detective and his ever-loyal partner. An Affair of the Heart demonstrates the critical interplay between the two men which made their partnership so memorable and endearing. The Curious Matter of the Missing Pearmain is a classic locked-room mystery, while The Case of the Cuneiform Suicide Note sees Dr Watson using his expert knowledge in helping to solve the mystery surrounding the death of an academic. In A Study in Verse the pair assists the Birmingham City Police in a complicated case of robbery which leads them towards a new and dangerous adversary. And to complete the collection, we have The Trimingham Escapade, the very last case the pair enjoyed together, which neatly showcases the inestimable talents of Sherlock Holmes.